Book Nineteen

The Empire's Gold

A novella from the saga of the Company of Archers.

"The kings of France and Venice believe the loss of the Latin Empire would weaken you and the Church to their benefit, Your Holiness. And to make sure it does, they are encouraging the Orthodox heretics and their Patriarch to retake Constantinople's throne. It seems they intend to divide the Papal States between them and become the two most powerful men in the world."

Was all that true? It could be. Who knows? But it was a very good story and had the fine merit of being confusing and blaming the French and Venetians for the Church's problems.

Chapter One

The Holy Father.

Commander Courtenay's meeting with the Holy Father went well. The Holy Father, Pope Honorius, was quite cheerful and beaming as the Commander approached the papal throne and kneeled to kiss the Holy Father's ring. I, as the Commander's new assistant, kneeled meekly behind him and remained there with my head bowed low throughout his entire meeting with the Pope. My knees hurt something fierce by the time it was over.

A number of clerics had been in the reception room when we were ushered into the Pope's presence by a grovelling young priest. All but one of the priests, however, immediately filed out of the room after backing well away from the Holy Father whilst nodding their heads towards him in elaborate bows and showing him the palms of their empty hands, probably so he could see that they were not carrying anything away.

The sole exception, the only cleric who remained, was a relatively young cardinal. He stood quietly next to the Pope and listened intently. The young cardinal bore a striking resemblance to the

Holy Father, except that he was not near so plump nor did he have white hair. From the looks of him, he was almost certainly the Holy Father's son or, perhaps, the nephew of the only man in the world who knew exactly what God wanted each of us to do.

It was all new to me. It was the first time I had ever seen a Pope or even knew his name or, for that matter, bowed to anyone other than old Squire Reynolds back home when he was drunk and ordered me do it. That was right before I told him to kiss my arse and ran away for an archer.

Pope Honorius was nothing like Squire Reynolds, of course. He was a large, elderly, and grey-haired man wearing a high hat with a strange shape and an elaborately embroidered robe that looked to be much too heavy for a reasonable man to wear in warm weather. His white beard was neatly trimmed and he sat on some kind of large elaborately carved chair and appeared to be quite friendly. His nose was normal, not anywhere near as big and red as Squire Reynolds's.

I had always assumed the Holy Father was so rich that he would be carried about in litter by the Church's slaves or ride to wherever he was going in a horse cart. But I could see that he must sometimes get to wherever he was going by riding a horse, but not often enough to toughen his arse. That was obvious because his chair had a big pillow for him to sit on to prevent his blisters from hurting. It was a fine idea and I resolved to get one for myself if I was ever assigned to the Company's horse archers.

The room where we were received by the Holy Father was the biggest and most impressive room I had ever seen. That, of course, was not saying much since the largest room I had ever previously seen or been in was the big tavern in Constantinople near the quay where the company's galley and transports tied up. It had especially good wine and the girls did not smell too bad if you got there early enough and the wooden window shutters were open.

The Holy Father's big reception room was definitely that of a very rich man. Its walls had canvas sails with all sorts of pictures of babies with wings painted on them hanging on them to keep out the draughts of pox-carrying air from the city, and a ceiling so high that a man could not come close to touching it even if he stood on a table and pointed his finger at the sky.

As soon as we entered the room, the Holy Father smiled at us from where he was sitting and beckoned us to come to him and kneel in front of him. Then he surprised me by welcoming the Commander in the heavily accented crusader French that people are starting to call English.

After his welcome the Holy Father immediately switched back to the church-talk called Latin and inquired about the health of the Commander's priestly uncle. He also asked about the state of something called the Diocese of Cornwall which the Commander's uncle had apparently purchased from the Holy Father's predecessor some years earlier. I was able to follow most of what he said because I had been learnt to speak and scribe Latin at the Company school.

The departing priests were long gone by the time Commander Courtenay finished explaining to the Holy Father about the current activities of his uncle and life in Cornwall. I, of course, did as I had been told. I averted my eyes, remained kneeling on the carpet-covered stone floor behind the Commander until the Commander stood up and motioned for me to so also. As you might imagine, all I did was keep my mouth shut and listen.

Both the Pope and the un-named young cardinal watched without saying a word when the Commander stood up and quietly placed a pouch of coins on a finely carved little table that was next to the little red pillows on which we had kneeled.

The Holy Father nodded his acceptance of the pouch, quite elegantly in my opinion, and we remained standing. Then the Holy Father and the young cardinal listened closely as the Commander gave his report.

Commander Courtenay told the Holy Father what he thought the Holy Father would want to hear—that the people of Cornwall all continued to remain completely faithful to the Church and went to their village churches several times each week to join their priests in praying for the Holy Father's health and safety.

It was not true, of course, because very few priests were allowed into Cornwall to sell their services, but it made the Holy Father smile and nod his head in agreement. In reality, of course, as everyone knows, many of our churches were only open when monks showed up to lead their prayers, the monks being more pious than priests and less likely to try to lure young boys and girls into the woods.

And then, with a great deal of sincerity in his voice, Commander Courtenay told the Holy Father what I was not so sure the Holy Father wanted to hear—that Cornwall's lands were so poor that the people had difficulty earning coins and feeding themselves.

"Unfortunately," Commander Courtenay said with a resigned shrug of his shoulders and a tinge of sadness in his voice, "the lands west of the River Tamar are so poor that many of the faithful are forced to become sailors or archers and leave Cornwall in order to earn their daily bread. It is the only way they can feed themselves and still be able to pay their tithes and buy the necessary indulgences for the evil things they do. It has always been that way. Even the Romans did not bother to build roads to Cornwall."

It was a fine story and helped explain why so many of the company's archers came from Cornwall and the nearby county of Devon, and almost all the rest came from England and Wales. It was also the same tale I myself was learnt to tell at the company school which was established on Cyprus two years later to teach scribing and summing to me and a handful of my mates, those of us who were willing to risk having our heads over-filled in order to gain promotion. It was also quite untrue since none of my mates and me, nor our families, ever paid tithes or bought indulgences.

After what appeared to be a brief and amiable conversation whilst the priests were leaving, the Holy Father's face turned deadly serious; he wanted to know the Commander's impressions of the Empress of the Latin Empire and her relations with the heretics of the Orthodox Church, the tithe-avoiding Venetians and French, and even the Empress's own nobles.

"The Emperor is still missing and I have heard disturbing reports about the Empress's behaviour as his regent from my nuncio and from the bishop who is temporarily administering the Diocese of Constantinople due to the pox that God has laid upon its Archbishop."

"Your Holiness, I am sorry to have to tell you this, but what you heard was coming from the mouths of men with foul motives and is almost certainly untrue. They have become overbalanced and put their ambitions ahead of the Church.

"In my opinion, the Empress is the Church's only true supporter from amongst the men you have mentioned. I believe the others are, in fact, likely to be telling false stories. They appear to be doing so promote their own personal enrichment and advancement, and to hurt you and the Church."

The Holy Father looked at Commander Courtenay intently—and made an impatient motion with his hand that he should continue. So he did.

"Your Holiness, it is an open secret in the east that the French and Venetians want one of the Church's enemies to seize the throne in Constantinople away from the Emperor XX and his regent, both of whom support you. Even worse, if that is possible, some of the Church's priests with ties to France seem to be actively helping them because they want to replace you with a French priest and move the papacy and Church to France.

"What the Venetians seem to want is for there to be fighting that weakens everyone so the Venetians can put their own king on the throne of the Latin Empire in Constantinople; what the French want is to weaken the Church so they can control the papal states in Italy and move the papacy to France.

"At least, that is what it looks like to me. I could be wrong, of course, but I do not think so."

The Holy Father seemed taken aback by the Commander's words. He became quite thoughtful and replied very softly after a long pause whilst he was thinking behind his eyes.

"You have given me much to think about, Commander, very much indeed," he finally said.

Then the Holy Father turned even more serious and asked Commander Courtenay about the cargo of coin chests we had carried to Rome from Constantinople. The Holy Father professed not to know the details of our encounters with the Venetians who had tried to stop us, and asked the Commander to tell him all about what had happened. He also wanted to know why the Commander thought the various events had occurred.

Commander Courtenay, of course, immediately began explaining what had happened, even though I soon got the impression he was merely telling the Holy Father what the Holy Father already knew. It was an exciting story, and even I who had been there in the thick of it learned quite a bit. The situation had certainly been more dangerous and difficult than my mates and I realized.

Despite what his spies might have learned from the slaves and Venetian prisoners we released, the Holy Father seemed to be genuinely surprised at some of the long and mostly true story the Commander told him about our recent fighting with the Venetians.

As you might imagine, and as was our custom, the Commander's tale was told in a merchant sort of way that would best serve the interests of our company. In other words, what he was trying to peddle something to the Holy Father that was neither complete nor accurate. The Commander, for example, did not mention that he had ordered the hanging of several men who were almost certainly priests after we had thrown the worst of the Venetians over the side as the bible requires of pirates.

When Commander Courtenay finished telling his mostly true story and answering the Pope's many questions, the Holy Father thanked him profusely and waved his cross at both of us to bless us for "fighting so bravely to protect the Church."

What the Holy Father meant, I subsequently came to understand, was that we were being blessed for fighting to protect the coin chests we had in our galley's cargo hold, the ones we had brought to Rome on behalf of the woman who ruled in Constantinople as the Empress Regent of the Latin Empire. I never did see her or learn her name.

My mates and I had never been told what the chests contained. But from their weight when we carried them aboard, and all the special efforts made to guard them, we had been almost certain they were filled with coins. We had talked about them constantly ever since we left Constantinople. Even so, I had not known for sure that the chests had coins in them until the day we reached Rome.

I only learnt for sure about the coins on the afternoon of our arrival whilst we were walking to the Pope's residence. That was when the Commander explained why we were visiting the Holy Father, and told me how I was to behave when we did—by kneeling whenever he did, not getting up until he motioned me to do so, and keeping my mouth shut.

As you might imagine, Commander Courtenay's immediate response to the Pope's thanks and blessing was all very proper even though what he said when he replied was, once again, not exactly true.

Instead of telling the Holy Father the truth, that we were only fighting for our lives and to protect our cargo because we had made our marks and were paid to always do so, the Commander once again did what was best for the company, he did what he had been learnt to do in his school—he told the Holy Father what he thought the Holy Father wanted to hear.

"It is always my greatest pleasure, and that of the men of my company, to be of assistance to Your Holiness and to your Holiness's loyal supporters such as the Latin Empress."

I, of course, solemnly nodded my head in agreement whenever the Commander did even though I did not have a clue as to what was being said since I did not know how to gobble the church-talk that I now know is called Latin.

And then, as you might also imagine, Commander Courtenay took advantage of the Pope's inquiries to bring the talk around to something that was always on my mind and the minds of my mates on our galley's rowing benches—whether there would be more fighting in and around Constantinople and how the company might be involved. In other words, he wanted to know about our chances of getting killed and earning prize money?

The Commander, of course, being an educated man who could read, and almost gentry even though his father had apparently started life as a serf, did not put things anywhere near so bluntly. He merely led the conversation in that direction.

"I share your concern, Your Holiness, that the French and Venetians might carry the Orthodox armies across the water to Constantinople in an effort to re-take the city and return the Patriarch and his heretics to power."

Commander Courtenay did not actually know, of course, if the Holy Father was actually concerned about losing his tithes and other revenues from Constantinople's Latin Empire. And I certainly did not.

But if the Holy Father was not concerned about losing some of his revenues and supporters, he should have been. It was clear to even me and my mates that the Greeks were forming armies to retake the city. We knew that to be true because we had just finished carrying the two largest Greek armies across the Greek Sea so they could fight amongst themselves for the right to lead the invasion of the Latin Empire and reap the profits that would result from its capture.

In any event, there were more immediate matters to be discussed. And the big one, of course, was the coins in the chests in our galley's cargo hold, the ones we had carried from Constantinople so they could be given to the Pope.

It seems the coins were intended as a "gift" to solidify the Holy Father's support for the appointment of Empress's second son to be the new emperor, if the rumours were true that her husband was dead, with the Empress continuing to sit on the throne as the boy's regent. At least, that is what the Commander had explained to me and Peter Lane, the captain of our company's shipping post in Rome, whilst we spent the better part of an hour walking from our galley to the Pope's residence.

Accordingly, I was not at all surprised when the Commander took advantage of the Pope's good feelings toward the company and brought up the matter of the coins our galley had carried to Rome. In other words, Commander Courtenay commenced negotiations for what I later learnt was the papal decree he had come to buy for the Empress. He began in a roundabout way by explaining what had happened so far. *I, of course, even though I could not understand what was being said, watched carefully as the Commander spoke so I could nod my head in agreement whenever he nodded his.*

"The Empress has employed some of the men and galleys of my company to help her keep the Orthodox armies of the Patriarch and her treacherous nobles away from Constantinople's walls, Your Holiness.

"And, I am happy to report, we have, at least so far, been somewhat successful despite our small numbers: We have temporarily delayed the arrival of the Orthodox armies and reduced their ability to hire mercenaries—by taking their coins in exchange for carrying them across the Greek Sea to fight each other for control of the Patriarch's army. In so doing, we caused them to waste their time and reduce their numbers.

"But now, it seems, the Orthodox princes have made peace amongst themselves under the direction of the Patriarch, and with the encouragement of the French and Venetians. It is sad to say, and I am sorry for having to report it, but the Orthodox princes are, as we speak, in the process of uniting what is left of their armies for the purpose of re-conquering the Latin Empire and diverting its powers and revenues to themselves and the Patriarch.

"The King of France believes the loss of the Latin Empire and its revenues will weaken you and the Church, Your Holiness. And to make sure that it does, he is encouraging everyone including the Venetians, the Empress's dissident nobles, and even the Orthodox heretics and their Patriarch, to try to take Constantinople's throne.

"Our spies report that, if any one of them succeeds, The French king and the Doge of Venice have agreed to move the papacy to France and divide the Papal States of Italy between them—and, in so doing, become the two most powerful men in the world.

"Unfortunately for the Empress Regent, many of the Christian knights and soldiers who would normally be expected to help her repel the heretics and her treacherous nobles have either been discouraged from doing so by the French and Venetians, or have gone for crusaders and are already doing God's work by fighting the Saracens at Damietta. The husband of the Empress Regent's daughter and his father are among them.

"The answer, of course, is many prayers for God's help and for the Empress to hire mercenaries to fight for her. And she is committed to doing so, hiring mercenaries that is, with all the coins she can beg and borrow in addition to those she has sent to you for your prayers and blessings."

There. Even I could see it. The chests of coins we had brought from Constantinople to "donate as a gift" to the Pope were out on the table, and the Commander had done it rather smoothly. It was effectively a request for the Holy Father to recognize the Empress's young son as the emperor and leave some of the gold and silver coins in our cargo hold for the young boy's regent, the Empress, to use to hire mercenaries to fight off the Church's enemies.

There were no flies on the Holy Father. He understood immediately.

"Ah yes, of course. She shall have my prayers and the support of the Church. Cardinal Savelli here will meet with you and arrange everything that is necessary. Thank you for coming to see me, Commander."

And with that we were dismissed and backed our way out of the room with many great bows and arm-waving gestures of submission. At least I think that is what we were doing as we left.

As you might imagine, Commander Courtenay had not told everything to the Holy Father. He neglected, for instance, to mention that the mercenaries the Empress intended to employ would all be archers and sailors from our company, and that he and the Empress had already made their marks on a contract to do so.

The Commander also forgot to mention that we had thrown the Venetian ambassador into the sea along with the Venetian pirates, or that we had hung the Pope's nuncio and the bishop of Constantinople because they had been with them.

It was reasonable, of course, for the Commander not to tell the Holy Father everything; the good man had enough on his mind what with having to talk to God and all. There was no need to waste his valuable time by plying him with additional facts.

Am I sure that was exactly what the Commander and the Holy Father said to each other and what it meant? No. I myself could not understand a word they were saying because I had not been learnt to gobble in the church-talk they were using. All I know is what the young cardinal who was present later told me. His name was Antonio Savelli and I came to know him and his priestly assistant, Father Simon de Brie, quite well.

Chapter Two

George has three meetings.

I had much to think about as my escort of six archers and I rode back to our galley in the warm sun of late spring. We did so in a couple of two-wheel horse carts. As a result, we were riding in comfort instead of having to walk as we had done to get to the Pope's residence earlier in the day when the air was much cooler and the streets did not smell so bad.

My new assistant, James Howard, had taken it upon himself to make the arrangements for the horse carts needed to carry us back to our galleys. They were waiting and ready to go as soon as we walked out of the Pope's residence.

James' arranging in advance for us to ride back to the river in the carts was a smart thing to do and much appreciated, and I told him as much. It meant we would not have to walk in the hot sun and once again risk fouling our leather sandals in the piles of fresh shite that the people of Rome go out every morning to deposit on the city's streets in front of each other's hovels.

He had hired them, the two-wheel horse carts in which we were riding, from amongst those that had been waiting for passengers on the street next to the Holy Father's residence. It was a good thing he did because, for some reason, I felt uncommonly tired after my meeting with the Holy Father. Who would have thought that talking to a Pope could be so wearing?

****** *George*

It was only fifteen or twenty minutes of cart-riding from the time we left the residence of the Holy Father until we made our way through the city gate and the Tiber River came into view. That was when I suddenly became aware that I was ravenously hungry. The feeling took me by surprise, particularly since I had broken my nightly fast some hours earlier, at sunrise, with a flatbread, some cheese, and a bowl of morning ale.

I had not initially realized how hungry I was until after we had spent some time bouncing over the rough cobblestones that paved Rome's crowded and narrow main streets. I had been lost in thought thinking about my meeting with the Holy Father.

Unfortunately, nothing new had come into my mind when I recalled our meeting and the Pope's response to the tales I told him. And then, somehow, my thoughts turned towards James Howard, my new assistant and fetcher, perhaps because he was sitting about two feet in front of me. As a result, I continued to remain relatively oblivious to the noise and activity in the crowded streets through which we were being carried.

Normally my assistant would have been a young apprentice sergeant newly graduated from my Uncle Thomas's school at Restormel Castle. And after his head had been sufficiently filled with knowing how to scribe, sum, and gobble in Latin, he would have been ordained as a priest so he could earn bread for himself if it turned out that he was not up to being an archer.

Harry Dunlop, the fine young man who had accompanied me from Cornwall as my apprentice sergeant, had been treacherously killed by the

Egyptians at Damietta. And then I had lost the apprentice sergeant who was Harry's replacement, Guy Falmer, when he received a well deserved promotion and was sent off to Cyprus as the captain of one of our Venetian prizes.

Being the company's commander kept me busy during all my waking hours. There was no doubt about it, I needed an assistant to run errands and fetch things for me. As result, I had selected James Howard from amongst the able-bodied archers who were still available on my galley after our fights with the Venetians. I did so because James had proved himself to be smart and alert when we fought our way past the Venetians to reach Rome.

James had been a good choice and was proving to be much more helpful than I would have thought possible. Normally, I would have promoted him and taken him on permanently as my apprentice sergeant with the expectation that he would learn enough so that someday he would become one of the company's captains, or even one of its lieutenant commanders.

Unfortunately, as things stood, I would have to find someone else to be my permanent assistant, someone who could better contribute to the company in the years ahead as a result of being my apprentice. My problem was that I could not adequately prepare James for promotion because he had a significant shortcoming.

It was not important that James did not know how to gobble Latin and mumble prayers as our apprentice sergeants were all learnt to do in Uncle Thomas's school. James, after all, had already proved himself as an archer. Accordingly, he did not need to be a priest and be able gobble in church-talk so he could earn his bread as a priest if he was not up to serving in the company.

The big problem with James was much more fundamental—he had never been learnt to scribe and do sums. In other words, he was just like almost all the rest of the company's archers and sailors. *All of them, actually, at least so far as I knew.*

James never being learnt to scribe and sum was a pity because, more than anything else, the Company of Archers needed men who could scribe and sum in order to successfully read and scribe such things as merchant contracts and coin transfer orders.

It was unfortunate, but all too true, that only a handful of young commoners, those who were being prepared to be priests and merchants, knew how to scribe and sum. The boys who were sent to become priests knew because they attended seminaries where they were learnt to scribe and sum by the older priests when they were not praying and being diddled in the woods; those who were to be merchants knew because they were taught by their fathers, or by tutors and scribes hired by their fathers.

The tutors and scribes the merchants employed for their sons were inevitably the same men the company was forced to employ to assist our post captains who had come up through the ranks and also did not know how to read and scribe—either defrocked priests who needed coins to buy their daily bread, and all too often liked being around young boys, or scoundrels who had been kicked out of their merchant families and priestly orders because they had become overbalanced as a result of too much learning finding its way into their heads.

A fine balance between being learnt and not being learnt the arts of scribing, summing, and fighting was needed because it was well known that a man can only hold so many thoughts behind his eyes at one time. I was always thankful that I had not been learnt too much such that I became overfull and could not perform. Even so, I knew I had come perilously close; some nights I had trouble sleeping because of all the thoughts swirling around behind my eyes.

So what should I do about James? He looked to be exactly the kind of man the company would want to have as one of its captains and commanders in the years ahead. But could a man who was already old enough to grow a beard be learnt to scribe, sum, and think ahead? Or would it weaken and overbalance him by making his head too full behind his eyes?

I did not know if it was possible for such a man to be learnt enough to be useful, of course, but I certainly knew someone who might. By the time our galleys were in sight I had decided to spend part of the afternoon scribing a parchment to send to Uncle Thomas in Cornwall.

In my message I would ask him what he thought about the Company setting up a scribing and summing school on Cyprus for those of our archers and sailors who might someday become our captains and commanders. And if we did set up such a school, how much of being learnt to scribe, sum, and look ahead did he think a grown man's head could hold before it weakened him and he could not think clearly?

Uncle Thomas would know such things if anyone would, being as he had read so many books and scrolls in addition to the bible and the parchments with the Latin words monks have to chant so their prayers reach God. That, of course, was many years ago when he was in the monastery before he rescued my father from being a serf and they went for archers with King Richard.

Hopefully, his head is not now so full that he cannot remember the words he read those many years ago.

****** *George Courtenay*

Cardinal Savelli showed up bright and early the next morning, much too early for me, in fact. He and a half dozen or so guards arrived when the sun was just coming up and I was standing in the stern of my galley yawning, half-asleep, and pissing into the river.

I was still groggy from my sleep and trying to decide whether to walk out on the long wooden plank of the galley's shite nest to poop, or go get something to eat from the cook, when I heard the sound of horses coming along the riverbank. A few moments later there was a shout from the sergeant commanding the file of archers who had spent the night on the riverbank to be our guards and watchmen against an attack by land.

"Hoy the deck; there be visitors."

The call came from Robert, a veteran sergeant, newly promoted to lieutenant who hailed from Duffield. He and his file of men were part of our first line of defence against anyone who might be tempted to have a go at us in an attempt to get the coins we were carrying. We did not really expect such an attack, of course, and particularly not by land, but we were ready just in case. One never knows what will happen when large amounts of coins are nearby.

It had been a cool, dry night, but already the air was warming for another hot spring day. I had had not yet broken my fast and was hungry. But the thought of eating before talking to Cardinal Savelli did not even occur to me; he was far too important and I was more than a little pleased to see him. I thought it a good sign that he had come so soon.

My hunger was instantly put aside and forgotten as I rushed to the deck railing and shouted out an invitation for him to come aboard. He did so, and brought a young priest with him. *An apprentice? Did*

"Good morning, Your Eminence. It is truly good to see you. I must admit that I did not think I would see you so early."

I gushed out my cheerful enthusiasm for the cardinal's visit as he climbed on to the deck of my galley and extended his ring for me to kiss. Up close, he looked somewhat wild-eyed and sinister with long stringy hair and a skinny body with arms too weak to pull a bow. His red cardinal's robe might have once been expensive, but it was now patched and dirty.

Cardinal Savelli, in other words, looked in the early light of the day more like one of the half-mad priests we try to keep out of Cornwall than a rich relative of the Pope or one of his friends.

"It is good to see you too, Master Courtenay. I came as soon as the prayers of matins were finished. I was called by God to come as soon as possible because we will be carrying out "God's Will" if we help the Empress stand firm against the misguided followers of the Patriarch and her other enemies."

"Exactly so, Your Eminence. I could not have said it better." *I truly could not; I just love it when doing what God wills is the same as doing good for the company's caches of coins. But does he really mean it?*

"Uh, Your Eminence, does that mean the Empress can keep her coins so she can use them to hire the mercenaries she desperately needs to hold off the return of the Orthodox heretics and discourage her enemies?"

"Of course it does, Commander, of course it does. Well, some of the coins, at least; the rest will be needed to pay for the necessary prayers. The Holy Father was quite clear that the Empress would be supported by both the Church and him personally. And I am pleased to report that his prayers will be free and numerous; only those from the priests and monasteries will be required. And joyfully for the Empress, the Holy Father himself will distribute them.

"That, Commander, is the very good news I have hurried here to bring to you. It means the Empress will be able use all the coins she can raise to hire mercenaries—except, of course, those that are needed to endow the necessary perpetual prayers in the monasteries and the expenses that will have to be borne to get them organized."

Except for the monks' prayers and the expenses to set them up? Damn; it sounds as if the decree will be costly.

"And how many coins do you think the expenses and the priestly and monastery prayers might require, Your Eminence?"

"Six thousand pounds of gold coins should do it, I would think."

I staggered back as if an arrow had hit me squarely in the chest.

"Six thousand in gold," I wailed incredulously. "Constantinople will be lost be lost to the heretics for sure. The Empress can hardly do that many coins in silver even if she borrows every coin she can borrow." *I was greatly encouraged; I thought he would start at ten or twelve thousand.*

"What if the prayers of the monks are not perpetual?" I asked with a shocked tone in my voice.

"Perhaps for only the next few years whilst she is seeing off the Patriarch and her traitorous nobles?"

After a few moments, whilst the cardinal was still pondering my question, I leaned forward and inquired further.

"Saving the Latin Empire would bring such a joy to God, Cardinal Savelli. Do you think the priests and monasteries could agree to five or six years of the necessary prayers for two thousand pounds, with another five hundred for expenses? She might be able to borrow enough to manage that."

"Impossible," said the cardinal as he gave me a shocked look and shook his head negatively. "Absolutely impossible. Five years of prayers would probably do it, but they could not be gotten for less than four thousand for the monasteries and fifteen hundred for expenses. You have my word as a soldier of Christ."

Then he with a look of pity on his face and sadness in his voice, he explained the situation and made a great concession.

"The monasteries already have to employ serfs and slaves because the monks spend so much of their time praying. If the monks have to spend even more time praying for the Empress, the monasteries will need at least four thousand so they can temporarily hire more serfs and slaves from the surrounding landowners. Moreover, the expenses to convince the monasteries' abbots to add the prayers to their monks already crowded schedules will be huge, far more than five hundred."

Cardinal Savelli had looked at me intently whilst he was laying out the Church's opening position and listening to my initial response. I, of course, kept a hesitant and aghast look on my face. As he spoke, I realized I was getting hungry and that it was going to be another warm day with the wind coming from the west.

It did not take much time before we agreed that a total of thirty-eight hundred pounds of gold coins or their equivalents in silver would result in enough papal and priestly prayers. Cardinal Savelli would, we both agreed, need another three hundred to cover the numerous expenses that he would have to bear. Other cardinals and priests would also have special expenses that would have to be covered if the total for the priests and the Holy Father was so low.

A few minutes later my new best friend and I went ashore together to the tavern next to the city wall to break our fasts and celebrate the agreement we had just reached. Our guards and assistants came with us. Everyone was pleased and smiling.

The agreement we reached was quite reasonable—three thousand pounds of the Empress's gold coins in exchange for four years of prayers from "enough priests and monks," and another twelve hundred his expenses and for the various additional "abbot-related expenses" that would have to be covered.

I was elated about the agreement, but took great pains not to show it. Of course I was pleased—our galley had more than twice that amount of the Empress's coins on board.

How many coins we had in our cargo hold was something I was determined to never reveal to any Churchman, or to anyone else for that matter. To the contrary, I intended , and did, pretend we did not have enough.

Keeping the number of coins we had available was a reasonable thing to do. There was no need for the Holy Father to know how well the Empress was doing at milking her empire. If he found out, he might try to squeeze more coins out of her instead of leaving them for her to share with us.

What sped up our negotiations was that we were both anxious to reach an agreement so we could go to one of the nearby taverns and get something to eat and drink to break our fasts. What had sealed the deal was a separate agreement wherein Cardinal Savelli would be paid an annual stipend each year to inform the Company on the Church matters that would be of interest to the Company. He would replace one of our previous papal spies, Cardinal Bartoli, who had recently gone missing.

James Howard and a young priest from the cardinal's entourage came to the riverside tavern with us. So did, Peter Lane, the captain of the company's local shipping post. As you might expect, I had to pay for the food and drink.

****** *James Howard*

I accompanied the Commander and the cardinal to one of the nearby taverns next to the city wall. When we got there, to be polite, I pretended to be hungry and ate some bread and a couple of boiled eggs. I did so even though I had already broken my fast by getting in the galley's food line early so I would be ready if Commander Courtenay needed me when he woke up. A young priest with an unsteady eye and a sore tooth came with us to the tavern. I knew his tooth was bad because I saw him wince when he bit down on a piece of bread.

An agreement of some sort had almost certainly been reached between the Commander and the cardinal. I was not sure, of course, because they had been gobbling away at each other in Latin. But I had seen them spit on their palms and shake hands, and afterwards they were most friendly towards each other and we had all gone off together to eat and drink.

Similarly, whilst we were eating I distinctly heard the word "bezants" and saw the cardinal make gestures towards our nearby galley. That was when I knew they were discussing the transfer of the coin chests we had carried from Constantinople. The young priest, Simon de Brie was his name, confirmed it when I quietly asked him, in crusader French, what was being said. He seemed a decent fellow and asked me many questions.

That morning was the first time I actually knew for sure that the chests held coins as my mates and I had always suspected. But the chests apparently did not hold enough coins. I learnt that when Father Simon murmured to me that Commander Courtenay had just told the cardinal he would need an extra day to borrow all the additional coins that their agreement required.

As soon as the cardinal and his men mounted their horses and rode off down the road that ran along the Tiber, Commander Courtenay sent me running off to fetch three horse carts and his nearby file of his personal guards under the command of Sergeant Williams. The guards and carts came quickly and we were soon clattering our way into the city with the cart carrying the Commander, the captain of our shipping post in Rome, and me leading the way.

I knew from what Father Simon had murmured to me as we ate that the Commander was going into the city to visit some of Rome's moneylenders. But I neither recognized the place the Commander named to the driver of our cart, nor was I told where we were going or who we were going to visit. And I certainly did not think it was my place to ask.

And one thing was now certain—assisting the commander of our company was very interesting and something that only a few days ago I would have

*considered beyond my wildest dreams; I was finally
sure that I had done the right thing by making my
mark on the company's roll and going for an archer.*

****** *James Howard*

The clattering hooves of the horses and the
sound of the wooden wheels of our carts on the
cobblestones were somehow soothing as we moved
through Rome. What came across to me as we
bounced and clattered through the crowded streets,
and people periodically had to jump out of the way to
avoid being run over, was that Rome was as big and
old as Constantinople, almost as crowded with people
and cats, and much dirtier.

On the other hand, Rome certainly had more
fountains and more statues of men who had died
many years earlier. I could tell they were statues of
ancient people because they lived years ago when
men wore no clothes and used tree leaves to cover
their dingles.

We were on our way to a place called "Trajan's
market." I had never heard of it or the rich man who

apparently owned it. That, of course, was not surprising since this was only my first visit to Rome, and archers like me were more likely to visit taverns and whorehouse than markets. Indeed, Rome was so large I probably would not have heard about the market even if I had visited the city many times.

About the only other differences I could see between Rome and Constantinople was that Rome seemed to have more priests walking about on its streets and slightly fewer cats to catch its mice and rats. And, of course, the people of both cities gobbled at each other in several different tongues, although that did not matter to me and my mates since we could not understand what was being gobbled in any of them.

Trajan's market was some distance from the river. And the streets were so crowded that it took us almost an hour to reach the market even though the drivers flicked their horses with their long whips and threw pebbles at them to make them trot whenever the street was open in front of them. We finally got there and climbed out of our carts just as my arse was starting to get sore from being constantly bounced up and down.

What we had reached was a tall and multi-floored stone building with narrow lanes beginning at each of its many street-level arches and running all the way through it. The street in front of the building was greatly crowded. There were horse carts, hand carts, and litters of all kinds waiting for customers, along with jugglers and buskers, barbers, and many foot merchants selling the services of women and small things such as apples and bowls of wine and water. It was also unbelievably noisy; everyone seemed to be waving their hands about and calling out to everyone else at the same time.

It was a large and impressive building and a conventional market all at the same time. As our driver pulled his horse to a halt, I could see the lanes into which each of the building's arches opened were lined with small market stalls that stretched all the way through the building to the other side.

We had no choice but to climb down from the horse carts and walk once we reached the noisy and bustling street in front of the market. Once inside we could see that the market's lanes were much too narrow for carts, and were packed with people looking for things to buy and merchants loudly calling out to hawk their services and wares. Cats were everywhere sleeping and washing themselves.

To my surprise, Commander Courtenay seemed to know where he was going. He walked briskly through the narrow lanes with such confidence that I was sure he had been there before.

We hurried along behind the Commander until we reached the stalls of the merchants selling gold and silver. Then we all stood silently and watched as the Commander bent down and whispered into the ear of one of the older merchants. The man nodded his agreement, said something to one of the other merchants standing nearby, and hurried away through the crowd.

A few minutes later Peter Lane and I were standing with the Commander at the rear of another stall and being plied with plates of fresh olives and bowls of wine. Sergeant Williams and his men stood nearby with their weapons ready in case of trouble. They were still not sure what was happening or why we were there. Neither was I for that matter.

I had just finished spitting an olive pit on to the dirt floor of the stall when Commander Courtenay said something to the sergeant commanding his guards and motioned for me and Peter Lane to follow him.

****** *James Howard*

A heavily bearded man wearing a little black cap on the back of his head led us to some stone stairs. The Commander and I followed the man up the stairs to a room above the busy market. The company's local shipping post captain, old Peter Lane, him what died of the pox the next year, came with us; the rest of the men were told to wait at the bottom of the stairs.

The room we reached at the top of the stairs had stones missing from one of the walls that let in light and a bigger opening in the same wall with the arm of a pulley hanging out from above it. It was obviously either a merchant's storeroom or a meeting room of some kind, or perhaps both.

There were three men in the room waiting for us. They were merchants for sure from the look of them. And two more men, and soon a third, came hurrying up the stairs right behind us. It was clear to everyone that it was a hurriedly called meeting.

Several of the late arrivals were red-faced and puffing when they arrived.

One of the merchants, their leader for that was what he surely was, immediately came forward and warmly greeted the Commander with a great manly hug and kisses on both cheeks. Then several of the others did the same and there were smiles all around. They were all wearing little black hats to indicate they were in the same merchant company just as we all were wearing the same light-brown tunics to indicate we were all men of the Company of Archers.

The leader of the merchants spoke first.

"It is truly good to see you again, George. I have been expecting you ever since I heard you had arrived with the Empress's coins and would be meeting with the Pope. So my dear friend, tell me how much more do you need for the Holy Father and how soon do you need them?" *Now how would a merchant be knowing that coins were needed for the Holy Father before the Commander told him? Of course, they must have spies in the Church.*

"Two thousand bezants with some of it in silver and copper so it will look to the Holy Father and everyone else as if we had trouble raising it. We will quietly repay it in gold within three days. Can you do it, Ezra?"

The merchant stroked his beard and turned to look at his friends. They nodded their agreement. He turned back to Commander and smiled as he too nodded. Then he spit on his hand and extended it.

"There will be no fee and one of the Church's spies will report that the Empress had to borrow some of the coins she needed to buy the Pope's approval for her regency. You and your company are friends, and friends take care of friends."

I understood the "no fee" since the merchants and our company were friends and we would only need the coins for a few days. But why did the Commander want the Church to find out that some of the coins were being borrowed? and why would the Church need spies if the Holy Father already knew everything from God? I had much to learn.

Chapter Three

The Beginning of Trouble.

As we rode back to the river after meeting with
the moneylenders I knew that it was time to turn my
attention back to my men and galleys. I had, quite
rightly in my opinion, left them in the care of my
lieutenants and hurried to visit the Pope as soon as
we reached Rome. I did so because I wanted the Holy
Father to hear my explanation of the recent events
involving the Venetians before anyone was able to get
to him with a different and less favourable version of
what had happened.

And my hurrying off to see the Pope seemed to
have worked. According to both Cardinal Savelli and
Ezra, the Holy Father had accepted my version of
what had happened on our voyage from
Constantinople. His willingness to accept what I told
him was helped, they said, by the tales being told
throughout the city by the newly released prisoners

and slaves from the Venetian galleys we had captured.

Their stories confirmed that we had been attacked by Venetians acting as pirates and, after winning a desperate battle, had ended up either hanging or throwing many of them over the side to drown.

I was thinking behind my eyes as to what I should do next when we passed through city gate and reached the road that runs along river. That was when I first saw, to my astonishment, the great crowd of people who had assembled on the riverbank next to our galleys. It was huge and it was growing; people were everywhere streaming towards the riverbank where our galleys were moored.

At first I was worried because I thought something bad might have occurred or still be happening.

"Whip them up, driver, whip them up. We need to get there fast."

Our driver could not understand what I was gobbling at him because I do not know how to gobble in Roman-talk. But he did understand what I wanted because of the tone of my voice and the fact I was standing up, pointing at mob standing in front of our galleys, and gesturing for him to a hurry. He whipped up his horse and so did the drivers of the cart following us with the rest of my men.

Everyone carrying swords drew them and all of our longbows were strung as we bounced our way along the river road. Our carts slowed down when we reached the edge of the crowd and were soon reduced to a crawl as the crowd slowly parted in front of us.

"Pay them off and follow me," I snapped to Peter Lane as I jumped down and began pushing my way through the crowd. My new assistant and my guard of archers were right behind me as I did.

What I had seen of the crowd as we approached, and more importantly what I had felt when we reached it, was that the crowd was large, but not at all unfriendly. In fact, some of the people in it were quite friendly and the rest were more curious than anything else. And, to my surprise, some of the people in the crowd appeared to be more than a little disappointed. My fears had been aroused by a false alarm.

On the other hand, our hurried arrival and our archers' tunics had been noted. As a result, questions and comments began coming at us from all sides as we began moving through the crowd. I could not understand a word that was being said to us, of course, but by the time I reached the line of sword-carrying archers who were holding the crowd back, I understood the situation, or at least I thought I did.

It seems our men who had gone ashore to drink and dip their dingles had somehow learnt of our cargo of coins. And so had the slaves and the Venetian prisoners we released. Their telling and retelling of the story about the coins and the Venetian efforts to take them, had caused the amount of gold coins we were carrying to grow and grow as the story swept across Rome. The people had come to the river expecting to see three English galleys so loaded with gold that they were in danger of sinking.

******

The state of affairs we found aboard our galleys when we finally made our way through the crowd was actually quite acceptable. Our galleys, and the men and coins on them, were neither sinking nor threatened. They had obviously been in safe hands whilst I was meeting with the Pope, the cardinal, and the money lenders.

David Black, my first lieutenant, and my sailing master, Alan Oremus, had risen to the challenge even though they were new to their positions. As a result of their good work, the slaves and prisoners had been promptly freed, our men had been given liberties with port coins to spend, and the food and firewood we would need to return to Constantinople had already been taken on board. We would get the water we would need from the river just before we sailed so that it would taste less foul than it otherwise would if it sat for days in our barrels and skins.

There was no doubt about it, we could cast off our mooring lines and leave at any time for Messina and Constantinople—if it were not for the coins we had coming from the moneylenders and the chests of coins we needed to deliver to the emissaries of the Holy Father. My lieutenants had done their duties in full even though they were new to them; I was more than a little pleased and told them as much.

Peter Lane, our shipping post captain, had also been most helpful whilst I was busy elsewhere. He had immediately mustered his men to serve as guards on the riverbank, and, as well, had engaged a couple of Greek physicians to barber our wounded and provide servants to care for them. Peter also found a hovel inside the city wall which could be used as a hospital and supervised the moving of our sick and wounded to it.

Moving our wounded ashore from the stern castles of our galleys where they had been sheltered and barbered, in turn, re-opened the castles for what was left of our sergeants and lieutenants to occupy. There were quite a number of them because of the recent promotions, and they were undoubtedly anxious to begin enjoying one of the most important benefits of their new ranks—a warmer and dryer place to sleep and a better place to shelter and huddle under their sleeping skins when there was rain and cold.

Whilst I was off to see the Holy Father, David Black and Alan Oremus had carried out my orders and released the slaves who had been on our prizes' rowing benches. They had also had freed the surviving Venetian prisoners so they could go ashore with slaves and join them and our liberty men in telling their tales about the efforts of the French and

Venetians to seize the coin chests we were carrying to the Pope.

Our efforts to influence the Pope's thinking seemed to have worked. According to both Cardinal Savelli and the moneylenders, the Holy Father had accepted my version of the events as being true. The cardinal was sure of it, he told me, because the Holy Father was quite upset with the French and Venetians and already begun talking to his close advisers about how he should respond to the attempts of the French and Venetians to reduce the power of the Church, meaning himself.

What more than anything else convinced the Pope and his supporters, I suspect, was that we had arrived with the coins destined for the Church and promptly offered them to the Pope. The details such as my falsely alleging the participation of the French king, and the hanging of a few churchmen who probably deserved it, paled in comparison to the basic goodness of what we had done and the coins we would deliver.

******

What was left of the day after my meeting with Cardinal Savelli, and then the moneylenders, was extremely busy and time-consuming. First amongst them was a parade and prayers for one of the wounded men, a newly promoted lieutenant, who had died of his wounds during the night.

My men and I could not leave the coins unguarded whilst we went to a church to pray over him, so I had his body brought to the riverbank, paraded all the men, and gobbled the prayers at him there. Then we put what was left of him in a new hole next to where we had buried our other men next to the city wall.

The crowd of people on the riverbank was very respectful throughout the service. They did not complain when we moved them back so there would be enough room, and stood silent whilst I used English to tell everyone what a fine fellow and good mate the lieutenant had been during his years with the company, and then gobbled the words of the Latin words needed to get him past purgatory without stopping for a visit.

And whilst all that was going on, one of our galleys had come up the river carrying a load of refugees and money orders. It also brought a couple of not very important messages and reports for me. One glance at them after the funeral service and I could tell that the news of our sea battles with the Venetians had not reached Cyprus before it sailed.

Unfortunately, the new arrival was one of our refugee-carrying galleys that sailed with less than a full crew of archers. Instead, refugees and other passengers were allowed to work off some of their passage fees by manning some of its oars. Even so, I promptly ordered ten of its newly arrived archers to temporarily move to the coin galley as reinforcements. They would replace some of the men we had lost in our most recent fight with the Venetians.

Additional reinforcements came from the dozen or so slaves and Venetian prisoners who had decided to stay with us for one reason or another instead of disembarking at Rome. We kept a few of them for service on the coin galley, and transferred the rest of them to the newly arrived galley to help take the place of the archers I had drafted out of it.

The plan was for the new galley to spend the day being resupplied and giving its men a night in Rome drink and dip their dingles, and then leave in the morning for Messina with Cyprus as its ultimate destination.

It would be just another regular voyage for the new arrival and its captain. My crew and I may have been busy fighting Venetians, but whilst we were doing so, and before we arrived, some of the men of our local shipping post had been going about their usual business of selling passages to potential passengers as well as accepting cargos and selling money orders. As a result, the new arrival would go out fully loaded when it cast off and began floating back down the Tiber in the morning.

The only tempest of the day came later in the afternoon and was quite mild—a quarrel between the two Greek physicians who were treating our wounded. One of them wanted to bleed our wounded men; the other did not. I decided against it and the would-be bleeder stomped away whilst muttering insults and angry comments no one could understand.

Not allowing the bleeding was an easy decision and one we had been learnt in my uncle's school; our wounded had already bled enough from their wounds and our captains were not allowed to bleed men who had already lost some of their blood. Bleeding was only allowed when our men were poxed and a physician said it actually might do them some good.

And, of course, one of the many things that needed to be done before we could leave Rome was deciding the fate of the two Venetian galleys we had captured. One thing was sure. We were not going to sell them in Rome because they would then almost certainly be bought up by merchants who would then either sell them back to the Venetians or sell them to the Moors.

Either way they would almost certainly sooner or later be used against us. Accordingly, we would follow our normal practice and either buy them in for our own use, so as to add them to the company's fleet of galleys, or we would burn them to prevent them falling into enemy hands.

Making a decision as to whether we should add them to our fleet, however, required a very thorough inspection of their seaworthiness, something that would take several days to complete and require a sea trial if there was any uncertainty. As a result, my lieutenants recommended that we let things slide and make no decisions until we could conduct a proper inspection of each of the prizes. I agreed.

Another reason we did not to start the required inspections was the arrival that afternoon of another of our papal informers, Bishop Agnelli. He showed up claiming to have important news, and insisting that I drop everything to meet with him and hear it in secret.

As a result, and over a bowl of wine in the very same nearby tavern where I had broken my nightly fast with Cardinal Savelli, I listened whilst the bishop confirmed what the cardinal and the moneylenders had told me earlier about the Holy Father's reaction to my story. He did so whilst bombarding me with questions about the coins and what had happened on our coin-carrying voyage. He also asked if I knew anything about a certain Cardinal Bartoli and Father Pantaleon who had mysteriously disappeared.

As you might imagine, I pretended to be totally ignorant about the missing churchmen and their fate. What I should have done, as it turned out, was grab Agnelli and make him tell me how it was that he knew about the missing priests, and why he was so interested in them. Unfortunately, it did not occur to me at the time. It turned out to be a serious mistake.

******

I was busy after I returned from my rather meaningless meeting with the bishop. I spent the rest of the day scribing a parchment to my uncle asking for his opinion about starting a scribing and summing school for our men, taking reinforcements out of our newly arrived galley, and meeting with my lieutenants and the captain of the newly arrived galley. I even found time to question a few more of the prisoners.

And then, when I finally retired to my bed in the forward castle, I somehow could not fall asleep. Instead, I stayed awake for quite awhile thinking about the women in my life and worrying about what I had *not* told the Holy Father—that the efforts to take the coins came from ambitious priests who wanted a French Pope and higher positions for themselves, and that I had hung them because they were responsible for the attacks that killed some of my men.

Exhaustion and the gentle rocking of the galley finally put me to sleep. And it was a good thing they did because tomorrow would be particularly busy and I would need to be fresh and especially alert all day: In the morning Ezra and the moneylenders would be delivering the coins we were borrowing, and then

Cardinal Savelli would be coming in the afternoon to hand over the Pope's decree recognizing the Empress's young son as the new emperor and take delivery of the coins for the monasteries.

Not that I believed for a moment, mind you, that a single coin would ever reach a monastery. It was merely a good story to justify the Church's rulers getting what they wanted without having to take up arms and becoming common thieves and robbers.

Chapter Four

The Big Surprise.

It was early in the morning and the line of galleys and dinghies extending out into the Tiber had come alive. Sergeants had begun sending their men towards the food that would break their overnight fasts, smoke could be seen coming up from the cooking fires on the decks of our galleys, and seabirds were circling overhead in response to the food being served. The more daring of the birds were known to swoop down and take a piece of bread or cheese right out of an unwary man's hand.

I ignored the birds as I rubbed my eyes to clear them whilst I walked to the shite nest in the stern of the galley to piss into the river. On the way I wished a mumbled "Good morning" to the cook and the men lined up for their morning flatbreads and cheese.

Everything looked and sounded quite normal as I did. It was a fine spring day. Our men were up an already moving about and beginning to engage in their various daily chores. The guards who had spent the night on the riverbank were being replaced by men who had already eaten. As a result, men carrying weapons were moving casually in both directions across the line of dinghies and galleys to get to their assigned places and duties.

Changing the guards on the riverbank required the men being relieved to step down from the riverbank into a dinghy, and then climb up to the deck of a prize galley being held away from shore by one of the two dinghies that were acting as a buffer to hold it away from shore. They would then walk across the galley's deck, climb down into another dinghy, and then up on to the deck of the coin galley where the cook had his flatbread fire going and was passing out bread, cheese, and bowls of morning ale. They would keep going and repeat the process if their destination was the second prize galley.

Their replacements, of course, did the same as they moved in the other direction. The result of so much activity was a constant bobbing up and down of the galleys and dinghies in the otherwise calm waters of the Tiber.

Everything was similarly peaceful and normal on the riverbank where the usual onlookers had already begun to gather. The lookers were a mixed bag: townspeople who had heard about the gold coins and probably wondered why our galleys were lashed together in a line that stretched out into the river instead of being moored along the riverbank, public women and their protectors looking for customers, early rising merchants and pickpockets seeking customers and victims, and men looking to sign on as sailors or to work their passages to wherever we might next be sailing.

Even though it was still early, there was once again quite a crowd of onlookers. And already lines of horse carts and hand carts were forming just beyond the crowd on the river road so as to be available to carry the people and goods who might want to engage their services. Everything appeared normal. It was going to be a particular busy day.

A few minutes later David Black, Alan Oremus, and I were standing on the roof the forward castle watching the people and activity and once again considering how the two coin transfers might occur.

We were talking about moving the coin-carrying galley to the riverbank when James came running up to announce the arrival of a messenger from Ezra, the leader of the moneylenders.

"I will be right there. Bring him on board and offer him a bowl of wine. And get me one too when you do, and flatbreads for both us."

Thank God it is almost over. I wonder if someone else could carry the decree back to the Empress. Then I could sail directly home from here instead of having to go back to Constantinople. It is already spring in Cornwall and my family is probably beginning to worry.

******

Ezra's messenger brought the news my lieutenants and I expected. The chests of borrowed coins had been assembled and soon would be on their way. The messenger estimated they would arrive within a couple of hours. It was time to get ready.

In between swallows of ale and bites of bread and cheese, I listened as the sailing master, Alan Oremus, began giving the orders to begin bringing some of the coin chests up from the cargo hold. We wanted them to be readily available so, later in the day, we could add enough of the coins we had brought with us from Constantinople to the coins we were borrowing.

I also ordered the dinghies and prize galleys buffering the coin galley to be removed so the coin carrier could be moved up against the riverbank. It would make it easier to load the coins we were borrowing, and make it less likely that any of them would fall into the water as they were being brought aboard.

******

The coin-carrying galley was in the process of being tied up along the riverbank when a desperate messenger staggered up and everything changed. He was out of breath and exhausted from having run all the way to report that the carts carrying the merchants' coins were under attack by a large band of heavily armed robbers.

According to the messenger, a man who had apparently been sent because he could gobble crusader French, some of the moneylenders had managed to take shelter in a nearby church and were holding the entrances. They needed help, he gasped out to me, and fast. He did not know the fate of the coins except that the robbers "were all over them when I was told to run for help."

Blow "to arms" I shouted across the deck to the galley's horn blower who was standing in his regular position on the roof of the stern castle.

Many of our men had seen the messenger coming and his disorderly condition. To a man, they had stopped what they were doing and were watching and listening intently. They knew something was up. Even so, it became a scene of absolute chaos as soon as I began shouting orders and my galley's horn blower began blowing his horn.

Men began running in every direction to fetch their weapons. Archers ran for their bows and began stringing them; sergeants and chosen men went for short swords and galley shields; and the cooks doused their fires and joined the sailors who were hurrying off to arm themselves with the galley's bladed pikes and swords.

"Archers from the commander's galley form a battle column by threes on the river bank," I shouted.

"Everyone else is to stay aboard under Lieutenant Black to guard the coins."

The sergeants and lieutenants, as was their duty, began loudly repeating my order. In my excitement I had forgotten that the men had not yet been told about the coins. Fortunately, enough of them knew about the coins and all of them knew what it meant to "stay aboard." As a result, my order was generally understood and obeyed despite my mistake.

I had jumped down from the roof of forward castle and begun moving towards the riverbank when the wild-eyed messenger arrived and gasped out his message. David Black and Alan Oremus had come with me and heard the message at the same time I did. They would stay behind to command the men guarding the galleys and coins.

My new assistant, Sergeant Howard, had started to come with us. But he turned around and ran for our weapons, mine and his, as soon as he heard my order for a marching column to be formed on the riverbank. The lieutenants continued up on to the riverbank with me to reach the messenger, and so did the galley's horn blower who was always supposed to stay near the ranking man on the scene.

The crowd of civilians on the riverbank initially remained and stared open-mouthed at the burst of shouting and frenzied activity that suddenly erupted in front of their eyes. Some of the crowd even pressed forward for a better look.

Everything changed in the crowd as seven dozen shouting and heavily armed archers suddenly began pouring ashore, and shouting sergeants and sword-waving lieutenants began pushing the crowd out of the way so they could form their men up into a battle column. There was a lot of confusion, probably because forming a battle column on land was something many of the archers and their sergeants had not done since they had been in Cornwall being learnt to be archers.

Within seconds the crowd was backing up, and then panic set in and many of them began running, perhaps thinking the archers were coming for them.

"Get back to the coins and take command of the galleys," I snapped at David Black just as James came bounding up on to the riverbank with a sword and shield for me. I was, as always, already wearing my chain and wrist knives under my tunic. James had both his longbow and mine slung over his shoulder along with three quivers of arrows.

Whilst all that was happening, the wide-eyed messenger desperately repeated his message several times. He had obviously run far and was totally exhausted, and yet I needed him to guide me to where the merchants were being attacked. That was when his sad state gave me an idea.

******

"Everyone who can is to climb into the horse carts; everyone else is to march along behind. Everyone is to keep their bows strung and slung over their shoulders. The men carrying swords are to keep them unsheathed."

I gave the order as I grabbed the messenger's arm to bring him with me. We ran through the crowd and reached the line of waiting horse carts just in time as their drivers were moving towards their horses and carts from where they had been standing together yarning. They did not have time to climb in them and gallop away.

"We will pay you double if you hurry."

I shouted my offer as loudly as I could. But I did not wait for a response as I jumped into the first cart to sit next to the driver and pulled the messenger up there to sit with us. James and Peter Lane climbed in the cart and so did four excited archers and the horn blower when I shouted and motioned for them to climb aboard and join us.

Within seconds there were ten of us squeezed on to the cart, or standing on its boarding step and holding on wherever we could. It was crowded since its two seats normally only carried no more than four passengers who sat facing each other. Then something important somehow found its way into my head.

"Peter, jump out and take command of the marchers. Follow us at the double. Commandeer carts along the way if you can. If you lose sight us, head for the Church of Santa Maria on the Via Flaminia. People along the way will know where it is."

I looked at the messenger as I named the church and street. He nodded his agreement that I correctly remembered the name of the church.

"The Church of Santa Maria on the Via Flaminia," Peter confirmed with a hasty shout as he swung down from the cart and ran for the column of archers rapidly forming up behind the line of carts.

"Go," I shouted to the driver of our cart after taking one last look at the carts and men behind us. "Whip them up, man whip them up."

The driver did not understand my English but he had nodded his head when he heard the name of the church and the street on which it was located. He knew it and where it was located.

What I saw as our cart lurched forward was quite encouraging; no one wanted to be left behind and have to walk.

Every horse cart behind us was packed with archers. They were squeezed in like fish in a sack. One enterprising young archer had climbed aboard one of the cart horses when he could not find a place to hold on to the cart; and every horse cart including ours had archers holding on to the outside of it or its horse's harness to help pull them along so they could run fast enough to stay up with us.

******

People stared, pointed, and hurried to get out of the way, as the cart horses, excited perhaps for the first time in their lives, thundered down the river road and carried us through the city gate. Our driver was loudly shouting and cracking his whip to encourage his horse and my horn blower was loudly blowing "attack."

Every archer was either in a cart or being helped to run alongside by hanging on to its side or the harness of its horse. People along the way watched and pointed at us in amazement, and scurried to get out of the way.

I was very excited—and so was everyone else including the horses.

Chapter Five

More big Surprises.

The Church of Santa Maria came into view as soon as the archer-carrying carts careened around a sharp corner and entered the little square on to which the church opened. What each of us saw as his cart entered the square was the scene of what had obviously been a recent battle. The door to the church at the other end of the square had somehow been battered open and there were armed men moving around in front of it.

Even more tellingly, wounded men were sitting and lying about in the square being tended to, and various unmoving bodies lay scattered about on the ground. There was an overturned and badly damaged horse cart on one side of square, but no sign of the horse which had pulled it.

****** *An unknown archer*

The horse carts that carried us clattered into the square with the Commander's cart leading the way. I was crammed into the cart right behind him, and Old Charley Carpenter, our galley's horn blower, was standing up next to me blowing *"Boarders Away"* and *"Attack."*

As might be expected, the men milling around in front of the church instinctively turned towards the noise and commotion of our arrival. Complete surprise and astonishment instantly showed on every one of their faces. We were definitely not expected.

A moment later it was as if an order had been given, and perhaps it was; the men in front of the church began frantically fleeing in every direction, including some of the men on the ground that were able to get to their feet and join them.

Others amongst the men on the ground tried to get to their feet and either failed or moved too slowly. And some of them were either dead or so seriously wounded that they made no effort at all.

One thing was instantly clear to all of us—the men in front of the church had no intention of standing and fighting.

"Take some alive. We need prisoners to question."

The commander shouted the order as he jumped down from the cart and ran for the door to the church with a short sword in one hand and a round galley shield in the other. Everywhere behind him sergeants were loudly repeating the order and men were hurrying to join him. I of course, was amongst them. It was very exciting.

As we ran towards the church, two men, one of them carrying a sword and the other some kind of club, dashed out of its open door and ran away down the adjacent narrow street. A moment later three more came hurrying out of a side door. They too fled.

Quite a number of my fellow archers, and the messenger who had come to fetch us, were right behind the Commander as he ran for the church's open door. Some of us were carrying swords, but most of us were archers with arrows already nocked into the bowstrings of our longbows. We neither stopped to deal with the men on the ground nor paid any attention to them. That would come later.

****** *George*

Our arrival at the church came too late. We found some of the moneylenders and their men alive, about a dozen of them, and several who were unmoving and appeared to be either badly wounded or dead. They were holding a defensive position in one corner of the dimly lit church with their swords drawn and their spears at the ready. As you might imagine, they were overjoyed to see us once they realized who we were. The coins were obviously gone.

Ezra was there. He was slightly wounded and kneeling by one of his sons who was dead on the floor next to him. Ezra, quite understandably, was distraught beyond words. It was all I could do to stop him from rushing out of the church to kill the seriously wounded robbers we captured when their friends ran away.

"No, my friend," I said as he picked up a sword and struggled to his feet. Murder was clearly on his mind.

"Not yet, Ezra. Wait and do that later. We need to question them first so we can find out who is responsible so we can kill them too."

I said it to Ezra at the same time I grabbed the arm of one of his spear-wielding servants who was already trying to push past me to get at the wounded robbers he could see through the church's open door. He was unwounded and clearly did not intend to wait. The church was increasingly full of excited archers who did not know what to do.

"Out. Out," I shouted at them. "Look for prisoners, lads, look for prisoners. We need them. Hurry."

Ezra finally came to his senses as the last of the archers hurried out of the church. He put the sword back down rose from where he had been crouched next to his son. He took a deep breath and looked around. There were tears and sadness in his eyes. His surviving men were beginning to put their swords and spears down and tend to their wounded.

"Yes, of course. Of course you are right. You are right. I will hold my vengeance until I bury my son."

Ezra's shoulders were collapsed in defeat as he repeated his agreement several times. He looked to be so exhausted that I feared he might fall down and sleep for a while.

A few minutes later, the glare from the sun caused my eyes to narrow when Ezra and I walked out of the church together. Curious Romans had already begun to gather and the windows in the buildings around the square were filled with onlookers. That was when everything changed once again.

Ezra and I had just come out of the church and begun to look at the wounded prisoners when another horse cart careened into the square. Out of breath archers who had lost their grip on the cart or horse they had been running alongside were still arriving when it galloped through the gathering crowd of onlookers so fast that it knocked one of them down and others had to dive out of its way.

"We are being attacked; we are being attacked." cried one of our new lieutenants as the cart pulled up in front of us. He was bleeding profusely from an open wound on the side of his face. He was one of the men who had remained at the galleys to help guard the coins.

Oh my God. We were tricked into leaving the Empress's coins unguarded.

******

The horse carts that had carried us to the church were still nearby because, fortunately as it turned out, their drivers were waiting to be paid.

"Back to the galley, lads," I cried. "Hurry. There is not a moment to lose. Let the marchers ride."

It was an order I need not have given. This time there was more than enough room on the carts because some of our men had followed my orders and run after the fleeing robbers.

As I swung aboard one of the carts with James Howard, the horn blower, and a number of archers quickly climbing aboard to join me, I had another thought.

"Leave now and whip up the horses. Do not wait for the men who ran after the robbers. They can stay and help out here when they return. *If they do return.* Hurry lads, hurry."

This time, at least, the archers who were available understood what was happening, and the cart drivers knew what we wanted them to do. The horses were still puffing and blowing when we once again began frantically boarding the carts. There was no time to wait for the return of the men who had chased after the fleeing robbers.

"Keep the prisoners alive, Ezra," I shouted over my shoulder as the cart driver whipped his horse into a lumbering gallop and we began moving across the square.

"We need to question them. Tell any archers who show up that I said they were to stay and help you."

My God. They tricked me into leaving the Empress's coins unguarded.

Chapter Six

A potential disaster.

Our numbers had been reduced by some of our men leaving the church square to chase after the fleeing robbers. We had started towards the church with ninety-one fighting men and passed through the city gate en route back to our galleys an hour later with seventy-eight. And we almost immediately lost nine more when the second horse cart, the one immediately behind the Commander's, overturned when it crashed into an oxen-drawn wagon that the Commander's cart driver had barely missed.

What we saw in front of us as we galloped through the gate was one of our prize galleys drifting down the river unattended with several bodies on its deck and a few men sitting and standing around them. There were also a number of empty small boats drifting along with it. In the distance, further up the river, we could see the other two galleys that had been in our galley raft—they were lashed together and surrounded by numerous small boats and dinghies.

Shortly thereafter, as we galloped up the crowded river road, we could see men on the decks of the two remaining galleys. As we got closer, the sounds of fighting could be clearly heard.

What my mates and I saw should have worried us because our lives would soon be at risk. But for some reason it did not; it was exciting.

****** *George*

People, carts and wagons were heavy on the road that ran along the river just outside the city wall. Most of them were hurrying in our direction in an effort to get away from the fighting.

Hearing our horn toots and seeing us galloping up the road toward them considerably alarmed most everyone on the road in front of us. They inevitably hurried to get out of our path. And, of course, everyone on the road seemed to be looking back to watch the fighting even as they scrambled to get away from it. They were not the only ones looking; so were we as we passed through them

But I was not thinking about the travellers on the road or the dangers of the battle my men and I could see ahead of us and were about to join. What concerned me was that I neither knew who we were going to be fighting nor why we were going to fight them.

One did not have to be a Greek physician to know that the raids were obviously intended to take the coin chests. That was certain. But there had to be more to it than that because hundreds of attackers were involved, and both raids happened at almost the same time.

So who arranged for so many raiders and gave the orders? And how would the raiders attacking our galleys fight when we reached them? At first that was all I could think about as our galloping horses bounced us up the river road to come to the aid of our fellow archers.

My thoughts changed as the sounds of the fighting began to reach us and I could see the decks and deck castle roofs of the two galleys. What I saw was somewhat encouraging; we may have returned in time.

One of our prize galleys was moored against the riverbank with the coin galley lashed to it so that it poked further out into the river. The dinghies that had been on either side of the prize galley to hold it off the riverbank and away from the coin galley were gone as was the prize galley that had been farther out into the river.

So far as I could see, most of the fighting was on the deck of the prize galley moored against the riverbank. But it certainly had not started there. The deck of the coin galley tied to it was strewn with what appeared to be dead and wounded men. There were also men who looked like archers on the roofs of both forward castles.

A number of dinghies and small boats belonging to the raiders were moored to our galleys. They were in addition to those we had seen floating down the river. The attackers had obviously climbed aboard our galleys without pausing to tie them up.

There was also a cluster of five or six of what looked to be our own galleys' dinghies tied up against the riverbank just below the scene of the fighting. *They were the dinghies that had been placed as buffers between our galleys to make it more difficult for would-be raiders to reach the galley in the middle that held the coin chests.*

The galley dinghies tied up together against the riverbank suggested that the attackers must have arrived whilst the sailing master, Alan Oremus, was in the process of carrying out my order to bring the coin galley to the riverbank to make easier and safer to carry aboard the chests of borrowed coins.

That the dinghies had been removed so that the remaining prize galley was now moored directly against the riverbank was important. It meant that it would be quite easy for my men and I to get on board the prize galley, and that we could board it from anywhere along the riverbank. It also meant we would not have to step down into a dinghy to get from the prize galley's deck to the deck of the coin galley.

As I jumped down from the horse cart, something important jumped into my head, at least I thought it was important: I realised that the raiders had arrived in small boats expecting to find the dinghies separating the galleys; they had not expected to find the dinghies gone and the prize galley moored against the shore and thus easily boarded from the riverbank.

In other words, hopefully, if I was right they had not expected to find our galleys moored so reinforcements could quickly get into the fight from the riverbank. So when they made their plans, they probably made no provisions to guard against the land-based counterattack we were about to launch.

I damn well hope they did not expect us to return fast enough to join the fight, or be able to quickly get on board to join it. We were going to be in big trouble if the leader of the robbers thought we might return and deployed his men along the prize galley's deck railing to prevent us from coming back aboard.

******

"Sound the call for a *boarding party attack*." It was the only one toot I could think to order.

I shouted the order to my horn blower as I jumped out of the cart and began running towards the galley moored against the riverbank. Archers were jumping out of their carts and following me. As I ran I shouted "Follow me," and "pick your man."

What my men and I saw as we rushed towards the fighting on the nearby galley deck in front of us was a ragged line of sword and shield-carrying sailors grouped together in a defensive position in the bow of the prize galley moored against the riverbank. In front of them was a much larger mob of attackers carrying swords and clubs. There was also at least one archer on the roof of each of the galley's forward deck castles.

Neither the archers on the roofs or those with our sailors appeared to be pushing out arrows. It almost certainly meant they had used up all their arrows. More importantly, the mob of robbers did appear to be pressing their attack on our survivors. They did not need to do so and suffer more loses; they already had access to both cargo holds and the chests of coins they had been told were in them. It was a standoff with the attackers free to remove the coin chests.

"Down. Get down," I shouted as I ran towards the galley tied up against the riverbank.

"Hit the deck; arrows coming. Hit the deck."

I shouted my warning in English as I ran towards the little band of our men who were holding one end of the galley. There was a very brief instant of hesitation, and then our men, almost all of them sword and shield-carrying sailors from the look of them, dropped flat on the deck. They knew what was coming; their attackers did not.

Our arrows began flying over the now-prone bodies of our men, and quickly cleared away the mob of raiders who had been confronting them. The raiders who had pushed our men into their smaller and more defendable position either took an arrow or ran. Some did both.

When I reached the railing of the galley, and was just about to jump over it, I suddenly realized how stupid I had been—I had been a thruster and charged forward in front of my men instead of with them. What would have happened to me if the raiders had had archers? Or if one of my archers had hated me or slipped and pushed an errant arrow out as he ran? My chain shirt might not have saved me at such a close range.

******

Many of the raiders responded to our charge and the cloud of in-coming arrows by panicking and running for their small boats to escape. Some of them got away. The others, however, made the mistake of waiting to run until we began picking them off with our arrows and swarming aboard the galleys. It was too late for most of them.

We quickly took the first the prize galley next to the riverbank, and then the coin galley lashed to it. Some of the raiders got into their dinghies fast enough and got away, but many did not. They either surrendered or died. And some did both.

The archers and sailors who had remained behind on our galleys, we subsequently learned, had surprised the raiders by giving an unexpectedly good account of themselves. That was probably because a handful of archers, those on each of the two prize galleys, had stayed behind when I rushed off to lead my galley's archers into the city to relieve the moneylenders.

Also amongst those who had remained behind were our shipping post captain in Rome, Peter Lane, and his four archers.

In the end, a surprisingly large number of our sailors and archers survived to fight another day, although some were killed and many were wounded and needed barbering. Only one jumped on to the riverbank and ran. Everyone else held true to their oath and stayed with their mates to help fight off the raiders.

Even so, it had been a close run thing. Our men held their own at first, but then the archers ran out of arrows and our survivors were forced to fall back into a defensive perimeter in the bow of the prize galley. That was where my men and I found most of them when we hurriedly returned.

Peter and Alan Oremus both survived the attack even though Alan was badly wounded and ended up needing almost a year of barbering in Rome before he recovered enough to return to duty. My lieutenant, David Black, was killed.

Chapter Seven

Aftermath.

There was much to do after we finished driving off the surviving raiders. We had men to barber and bury, prisoners to guard and question, and a galley drifting down the river to recover. And looming over it all was the huge payment I would soon have to make to cover the cost of the prayers that were needed so God would choose the Empress's second son as the rightful emperor in Constantinople with the Empress as his regent.

As I went about my post-battle duties, an important question increasingly filled the space behind my eyes—should I use some of the Empress's coins in my galley's hold to make up for the coins we had intended to borrow for a few days from Ezra and his friends?

It was an important question because the Church's demands on the Empress would be lower in the years ahead if the Holy Father and his priests could be gulled into believing the Empress was so poor that she had to borrow money—and that would leave more coins for us to be paid for defending her.

****** *Post Captain Peter Lane*

Due to Alan Oremus, the coin-galley's sailing sergeant, being badly wounded and suffering great agonies that required him to eat large amounts of flower paste to sooth himself, it was Commander Courtenay himself who sent off some of our able-bodied sailors in the attackers' dinghies to retrieve our missing prize galley, the one that had somehow come unmoored during the fighting and had last been seen floating down the Tiber.

A few minutes later, whilst we were still picking up our dead and wounded from the galley decks and giving flower paste to those of our men who were in great pain, the Commander ordered me to send one of my post's three surviving archers, Dick Fisher, to find out what was happening at the Church of Santa

Maria, and another, Harry Hayward, to summon physicians and barbers for our wounded.

Most of the captured raiders were wounded and some of them were treated roughly by our men after they were captured. But we mostly left them where they fell or had managed to drag themselves. No efforts were made to either torture and kill them, or ease their pain with flower paste.

As a result of our initial benevolence and generosity in not mistreating them, something that they themselves would almost certainly not have done if our positions had been reversed, our prisoners seemed to consider themselves lucky and grateful for being alive despite the pain of their wounds. Indeed, several of them seemed to be saying as much to us even though no one could understand what they were gobbling.

One thing was certain however; they would not have been of such good cheer if they had known how the bible requires pirates to be treated, or that they were about to be seriously questioned. But I could see that one of them needed to be questioned immediately and suggested as much to Commander Courtenay

"Commander, I recognize the prisoner over by railing, the one with the arrow in his belly who wakes up and starts screaming every so often. His name is Antonio. He is the captain of our parish church's local protection gang. They meet and drink at the tavern down the street from our post.

"I am sure that is who it is. He came to me with a couple of his men when he first became the head of his gang and demanded that I give him a silver coin each month for his gang's protection and some prayers for my soul by the priests in the parish church.

"Very threatening he was until he understood that our company never pays for protection and its post captains like me do not have any coins of their own to do it themselves and would be immediately replaced if I used the company's.

Peter smiled and added an even better explanation.

"It also probably helped when I told him that if anything happened to me or the post, the commander of my company would almost certainly arrange to have him killed most horrible in order to encourage his mates to stay away. Believe it or not, we actually became a bit friendly after that, and even had a few bowls of wine together. It seems people rarely turned down his gang's offer of protection and the inability to collect from our company impressed him."

Then Peter turned deadly serious.

"One of the archers got him with an arrow early on. In his gut. So you best question him as soon as possible. He is not going to last much longer."

"Is he now? Antonio you say? Ah yes, you are right, captain, thank you. I will get to him as soon as I finish passing out flower paste to our wounded lads."

And giving a mercy to one of my men who will not make it—the commander's duty I most hate.

****** *George Courtenay*

I knelt down on the deck next to where Antonio had dragged himself, and told my lies as I asked my questions in crusader French.

"Antonio is it? Your men told me that is your name so I suspect it is true, eh? Would you like the arrow removed and some water and some flower paste for your pain?"

One of recently released Venetian slaves knew how to gobble Italian. He knelt down next to me and translated. Antonio was lying on his side on the deck panting and holding on to the goose feathers of the shaft protruding from his stomach as he gobbled back at me with many grimaces and groans. He was sweating profusely but, strangely enough, not bleeding.

"Please help me. Please signor. Oh God, I need a barber."

"Of course you do, Antonio, of course you do. And we will get one for you, and the pain will end, as soon as you answer my questions. I promise. But first I need your answers so I can confirm what your men and others have already told me. Who ordered you to attack us? What is his name and what did he tell you?"

I was telling him lies, of course. Antonio was the very first of the prisoners I would question. The others could wait until later in the day after we delivered the coins. For Antonio, however, it was obviously a now or never situation—one of the newly arrived Greek physicians had shaken his head and said "probably not" when I asked if he would live for a few more hours so I could question him later.

An anxious archer was hovering nearby as I finished my questioning. He wanted his arrow back. The questioning had taken quite a bit of time, too much in fact, because Antonio kept closing his eyes and falling asleep, and having to be awakened by gently shaking the arrow.

I had learnt much before I let the archer pull his arrow on through and throw Antonio into the river to end his pain and horrible screeching and wailing. I had a lot to think about when I stood up and began giving orders.

****** *Commander Courtenay*

We threw the dead raiders into the river and moved our own dead and all of the wounded men, both theirs and ours, to the remaining prize galley, the one moored against the riverbank. And since it was doubtful that another raid could be organized so soon, I had the coin-carrying galley moved to the riverbank so the coin chests could be more easily and safely unloaded. It was definitely the right thing to do as dropping one of the chests into the river would cause no end of problems.

The coin-carrying galley was still in the process of being tied up slightly downstream from the prize galleys when Cardinal Savelli and Father de Brie arrived to collect the Empress's coins. They were early and had come with what must have been an entire company of papal guards, a gaggle of priests and monks to watch over the coin counting, and a half a dozen horse-drawn wagons.

"We are taking no chances as you can see, Commander. We have brought a full half of all the papal guards with us in case the robbers decide to strike again."

"It is good you did, for we have the coins waiting for you and it seems that a lot of people want them."

Cardinal Savelli's eyes opened in surprise when I told him he would get all the coins required by our agreement. *Now why is that? How did he know so quickly that the moneylenders' coins had been stolen?*

"We borrowed the additional coins we needed from another company of moneylenders after those of our first source were lost to robbers," I told him. *And that was somewhat true—we borrowed them from the coins in our cargo hold that would have been used to repay the moneylenders in a couple of days.*

"And may I please have the Holy Father's decree so I can make sure it is what I have been ordered to obtain." *Notice how tactfully I put it? Uncle Thomas would have been proud.*

A round messenger's pouch was promptly handed to me, with a smile, by Father de Brie. The pouch was made of leather and had a leather cap to protect its contents from water and mice.

I pulled the decree out of the pouch, unrolled it, broke the wax seal, and began reading. As I did, I motioned to the sailors to begin moving the chests from where they were stacked to the bow of the galley where they would be counted. Some of the sailors seemed to be quite impressed that I could read.

Cardinal Savelli and his men had arrived and handed me the decree whilst the coin chests were still being taken out of the cargo hold. At my signal, our sailors began carrying the chests from where they had been initially stacked on the deck to an open area in the middle of the deck where the coins would be counted. Once counted, the sailors would then carry them ashore for the papal guards to load on to their wagons.

The decree itself was quite flowery, but straightforward and appeared to be correct in all ways. I bowed my acceptance and tucked it under my arm after I slowly and carefully read it several times. A few seconds later I held my hand out for carrying pouch and left it out until Father de Brie silently handed it to me. Then the three of us stood, silently for the most part, and watched until the counting of the coins and the transfer of the chests was completed.

Everything went smoothly after a very brief delay. The delay occurred when the chests were opened so the coins could be counted into the empty chests that had been set out on the deck for just that purpose. The coin chests that were emptied as their coins were counted would then be used as the next empty chests to be filled as more coins were counted. That was my plan.

"Oh, counting is not necessary at all, Commander, not necessary at all. The Holy Father trusts you and so do I."

"As I trust him, of course I do; he can do no wrong, can he?" was my response. *Actually, I am not so sure about either of you.*

"But I must insist on counting them so everyone can see that they are all there. I need to do so, count them that is, to protect my honour and the honour of my company; what if someone miscounted when the coins were being placed in the chests, or someone was able to get into the chests and take some of the coins when we were not looking?"

I stood firm on my insistence for a very public counting. As a result, the coins in each chest were counted for all to see, including the great crowd of people who had once again gathered a few steps away on the nearby riverbank.

After the coins in each chest were counted into an empty chest, the new chest was immediately taken ashore and loaded on to one of the wagons. The cardinal's several efforts to stop the counting, "because I believe you and have other things to do," were ignored. *But they certainly raised my suspicions; why did he keep trying to stop the counting?*

Although the good cardinal did not know it, his efforts to hurry things along, by stopping the counting, seemed to amuse Father de Brie as much as they concerned me. I saw him smile to himself, when the cardinal was not looking, and nod his agreement to my insistence on continuing to count the coins. It struck me as a bit strange.

Of course I had the coins counted so everyone could see them, including the mob of curious onlookers who had once again gathered on the riverbank. I was dealing with priests whose desire for coins was well-known. There was no way I was going to take a chance on the decree being revoked because someone subsequently claimed to the Holy Father that we had cheated him.

******

It took a while to count out the coins, but the transfer was completed and Cardinal Savelli made his mark on a parchment receipt. After the coins and churchmen departed, I turned my attention back to the report I had received from Ezra and to our dead and wounded men and our prisoners.

Ezra's message confirmed what I had heard from Antonio and our other prisoners—our attackers were members of some of the city's church-sponsored protection gangs, the men who helped the city's company of vigils keep order in that area of Rome that is their church's parish. It was the same system in use throughout the Christian world wherein each parish had its own gang of men to protect its faithful from those who would harm them—and, of course, whether they actually protected the parishioners from robbers or preyed on them, or both, depended on the bishop who ruled over the priests serving in that particular parish.

One of the things I learnt from the prisoners I questioned surprised me and also worried me because I was not sure of its significance. It was that each of the churches in Rome was considered to be a separate diocese and led by cardinal-bishop who chose its priests and collected its revenues from its property rentals, donations, indulgence sales, and protection services. *As I later discovered, it was the way the Holy Father paid the church's cardinals to stay in Rome and help him run the Church.*

"It was not personal; it was business," Antonio had gasped. "We did not attack because we hate you, but because we were ordered to do so by our cardinal, Cardinal Nardin. He lied to us; he said it had been arranged so that only a few sailors would be on board."

It was breath-taking information. So far as I could tell, the men from at least seven of Rome's parish protection gangs had been involved in the two attacks. It meant that as many as seven of the Church's cardinals had approved of the attacks. But why?

And then, whilst I was still questioning Antonio, an alarming thought began to creep in behind my eyes with a second question—could it be that the Holy Father himself ordered the raids using the Church's protection gangs because he wanted the coins, but did not want to recognize the Empress for some reason?

It was a possibility that was hard for me to believe. And yet the Popes were always tricky and devious Italian priests according to my uncle. He said they had to be that way in order to buy the votes needed to be elected to Saint Peter's throne and become the only living man who was able to talk to God and understand what God wanted everyone to do.

But what did it mean that so many cardinals
were involved? What should I do?

Chapter Eight

Prayers and Lamentations.

I was tired the next morning due to a lack of sleep. It was understandable; the candle lantern I was using had been lit for hours by the time I finally finished questioning the prisoners and made my way to bed. And then, well before dawn, after a somewhat sleepless night of thinking about what I had heard and what I should do, the arrival of another messenger from Ezra resulted in me getting up much earlier than usual.

On the other hand, after I got up to listen to Ezra's messenger, I realized that my night of tossing and turning had settled the uncertainty that filled my mind and kept me awake—I had decided to delay my sailing for Constantinople.

It was a significant decision. It meant the Empress would have to wait a day or two longer to receive the Pope's decree. It was a decision I reached after spending most of the night in bed thinking about the prisoners' answers to my questions. The cryptic message I received from Ezra merely solidified my decision to wait.

Accordingly, instead of leaving for Constantinople immediately after we buried our dead, we would remain in Rome for another day or two whilst I talked with the moneylenders and dealt with the men who had ordered the attack which had killed and wounded so many of my men. But how?

******

Ezra's messenger had arrived early in the morning when it was still dark. And, since God was not watching over me as well as he might, Ezra's messenger arrived in time to wake me just after I had finally fallen asleep.

But I had been happy to see him despite the hour—because what he whispered to me was that Ezra had obtained some important information he wanted to share with me personally. As a result, according to the messenger, Ezra begged me not to sail until we had a chance to discuss it.

Unfortunately, Ezra's messenger, a man named Abraham who had apparently been selected because he could gobble crusader French, had no idea as to what the important information might involve. All he knew, Abraham said, was that Ezra was in mourning for his murdered son, and that his taking time to send a message to me meant the information he had was likely to be quite important. I agreed. It certainly sounded that way to me.

I had already decided to visit Ezra to pay my respects for the loss of his son. Now, as a result of his message, I decided to visit him immediately after my men and I buried our dead and visited the tavern which Antonio's gang was known to use as its meeting place.

The tavern and church were both down the street from our shipping post so I knew exactly where to find them. Hopefully, the church's high priest, a cardinal, would be there so he could help me with my inquiries.

And immediately after visiting Antonio's haunts and Ezra, unless Ezra's information suggested otherwise, my men and I would work our way back to our galleys after visiting the meeting places and churches of some of the other gangs whose men had attacked us.

In each case, although my men did not know it, and I certainly did not inform Ezra's messenger, we would also be visiting the priests of each gang's church to hear *their* prayers, confessions, and offers of penitence. With a little bit of luck we might even find their high priest, their cardinal.

I knew my men would be pleased with what I had in mind. And, with a little bit more luck, we would all be well compensated as well.

Ezra would also be pleased with what I hoped to do in the way of vengeance, of that I had no doubt. With that in mind, I asked Abraham, his messenger, to remain on board so he could guide me to Ezra later in the morning. Alternately, if he needed to ride back to report to Ezra that his message had been successfully delivered, would he please, I requested, return after he gave his report. I needed him to guide us to Ezra after we visited our other destinations.

Abraham said he needed to ride back to report, but agreed to immediately return to help guide us to Ezra's residence or wherever else in the city we might want to go. I did not in any way suggest where that might be.

******

After Abraham left, and whilst I was still drinking a bowl of ale and eating scrambled eggs and bread to break my fast, I ordered Antonio's body to be fished out of the river from where it had come to rest up against a bush protruding from the riverbank.

It took some doing, but what was left of Antonio was soon back on board. A few minutes later, when I saw that my men had finished eating, I had my horn blower blow on his horn to call everyone to assemble on the coin-galley's deck. It was time to perform the commander's duty I hated more than almost any other. *The only one worse was giving a mercy to one of my men.*

When everyone except those of our men who were too wounded to be moved was lined up on the deck, one of the lieutenants ordered "hats off," and I began gobbling the Latin words needed to properly send our dead to heaven without having to stop to burn for a while in purgatory.

It was a sad occasion and many of the men, including me, were overcome with grief at times, or at least pretended to be as expressions of grief were expected and thought to be respectful. There were twelve of our men dead who needed praying over including a sailor who had died quietly in the night a few hours earlier.

The funeral service itself went particularly well, probably because the day was not yet too warm and I was able to remember most of the required funeral prayers and chants. As usual, I filled in with some baptism prayers when I was unable to bring the missing funeral prayers into my head fast enough.

All in all, the service was adequate even if my prayers were not great. My men appeared satisfied, and the large and growing mob of onlookers and hawkers on the riverbank seemed impressed even though not a one of them could understand a word of Latin or English.

After I finished gobbling the required Latin prayers, the mates and friends of our fallen took turns saying a few words of remembrance about each man as was our tradition. It took some time because we had lost so many men.

Each man who spoke told everyone what a good mate one of the dead men had been, and how much he would be missed. We all nodded our heads as he spoke even though what was spoken and remembered were only the good parts of his life. The bad parts were overlooked as was the Christian custom; they would be interred with his bones and forgotten.

When everyone who wanted to speak had finished, I gobbled one final prayer in Latin and that part of the burial service was completed.

Immediately afterwards, with a drum slowly beating, we solemnly carried the bodies of our dead ashore on their own sleeping skins with one man holding each corner and another on each side holding the skin in the middle. They would be buried together, with their arms linked together, in a hastily dug trench next to the city wall.

When we reached the trench, I stood by it and chanted Latin as the bodies were gently placed in the trench and arranged side by side by men who were rarely gentle. Then, whilst the dirt was being thrown in to cover their bodies, I gobbled one final prayer that no one could understand, listened whilst the horn blower tooted something mournful, and then said a few words in English that seemed to please everyone in attendance.

First, I announced that a remembrance stone would be put on the nearby city wall so they would not be forgotten. That got some nods and murmurs of appreciation from the men.

Then, to the accompaniment of many growls of agreement, I loudly reminded everyone who had survived that the company's charter required great revenges when someone on the company's roll was killed or wounded.

After that, I turned to the men and made a promise. With fire and brimstone in my voice, and whilst repeatedly stabbing my pointing finger at the sky for emphasis, I told them what to expect.

"I am determined that our revenges will be even more terrible than our company's charter requires, and they *will* begin immediately."

The men cheered and jumped about.

******

I was satisfied as we walked back to the nearby galley. All in all, the funeral service and burials had gone well. By the time our praying and reminiscing was finished, we were all thirsting for revenge despite most of us not wanting to fight and take a chance at getting killed. *An arrow from a safe distance or a stab in the back is always best, but sometime fighting face to face cannot be avoided.*

After brief pause lasting a few minutes whilst everybody pissed and the archers fetched their bows and swords, a dozen or so tightly bound prisoners whose questioning had been completed were thrown into a hastily rented horse cart with what was left of Antonio on top of them. Then off we marched to visit the tavern frequented by Antonio's gang, and then Ezra and the moneylenders.

Another wagon led the way. It carried several candle lanterns in addition to some of the other things we would need and three of my galley's sailors who knew how to climb rope ladders and hang sails. The candle lanterns were lit in case we needed a readily available flame to burn something down.

The people who had gathered on the riverbank to watch us knew something was about to happen when they saw us form up into a marching column carrying our weapons. But they had not a clue as to what it might be, and neither, for that matter, had my men or anyone else—for I had told no one what I had in mind, not even my surviving lieutenants.

What the watchers and my men also did not know was that I had begun scribing two lists and had brought a copy of one of them with me to share with Ezra. The lists contained the names which had been given to me by some of our prisoners, albeit sometimes reluctantly, when I questioned them.

One list contained the names and descriptions of the men and gangs who had attacked us on the river and were thought to have gotten away; the other had the names and descriptions of the "big men," all cardinals, who had ordered them to do so.

I had to share something with Ezra so I decided to give him the list with the names of some of the attackers who had gotten away; the names of the "big men" who had committed treason against the Pope would stay with me until I decided how best to use them.

They were good lists. Hopefully, I would be able to add more names to them later today and in the days that followed. But then what? It was a question I could not answer.

* * * * * *

A column of more than seventy archers marched through the city gate with the wagons carrying the prisoners and our supplies and sailors following close behind. We marched to the booming beat of a marching drum with resolution and determination on every man's face.

It was my intention to continue to march in such a manner almost all the way to the tavern Antonio's gang was known to frequent. Our shipping post captain, Peter Lane and Abraham, Ezra's messenger, marched beside me at the head of the column. James Howard and my galley's drummer and its horn blower marched immediately behind us.

My men, including my lieutenants, still had no idea as to where we were headed as we passed through one of the unguarded river gates in the Rome's great city wall. But they had somehow come to understand that the company's vengeance was about to begin. Perhaps it was fact that some of the prisoners were with us and the nature of the equipment and supplies we were carrying that informed them.

It took no more than fifteen minutes to march three abreast to our shipping post. The tavern which was our first destination was about four hundred paces on past our shipping post. It was on down the slightly curving street at the next corner.

As you might expect, our marching drum, our periodic marching chants, and the slapping sound as our sandaled feet came down together attracted the attention of people both in the narrow street and in the window openings above it.

People saw us and heard us. And, once they did, almost everyone stopped whatever he or she was doing and stared. They did because we looked like what we were—a battle-ready company of determined and heavily armed fighting men looking for a fight.

It was no surprise at all that many of the onlookers made the sign of the cross when they saw us up close, and those who found themselves in our path hurried to get out of our way. As usual, the "Vigils" who were supposed to keep order in the city were nowhere to be seen. Their luck was holding.

Seeing us was what I wanted, of course—so the word would get around the city and through the Church that the English Archers and their company were not ever to be trifled with or ignored. As you might imagine, our march through the city was just the beginning.

******

The tavern at the corner of the crossroads ahead of us was not much to look at. It was just another rundown local tavern on a shabby corner where two narrow streets came together. Narrow slits fairly high on the wall along the street let in light when the large window openings all along the street were closed. Its main entrance door was on the corner where the streets came together. It was altogether conventional; most neighbourhood taverns in large cities had such an entrance where two streets came together. They also usually had another smaller door in the rear.

I had already stopped the drum when I halted the column at the entrance to a narrow alley just past our shipping post and what looked to be about the four hundred paces short of the tavern where the members of the parish's protection gang hung out.

"Lieutenant Crawford, take six men down that alley and try to find the rear door to that tavern up ahead on the starboard side of the street. Do not let anyone in or out of the tavern. Stop anyone who tries to force his way past you even if you have to kill them; otherwise just turn back anyone who tries to escape and leave them unharmed. Come back here if there is no door."

We stood leisurely at ease in our ranks and waited a couple of minutes to give Crawford and his men enough time to get in place and for the men in the column to relieve themselves by pissing against the wall of a nearby hovel. Whilst we waited, we saw several men come out of the tavern and walk away.

After a few minutes, when I thought the men I had sent around to the rear might be in place, I ordered most of my men to tread quietly and follow me up the street to the front door of the tavern. Only a few archers were left behind to guard the prisoners and the two wagons.

I gave the men their orders before I started walking casually up the street.

"We are going to let any women and children leave and we are going to stand far enough back from the door of the tavern up there so that the men inside it can come out and look around."

As I had hoped, the residents of the gang's neighbourhood and the people walking in the street stopped whatever they were doing and watched as we quietly walked up the street towards the tavern. The window openings in the daub and wattle hovels along the street began to fill up with watchers.

There was an ever increasing number of people pointing and talking to each other in muted voices as my men and I quietly moved up the street towards the tavern where the gang members spent their idle hours.

******

I could somewhat see into the dimly lit tavern as I walked past the window openings in its wall. There were a number of men sitting and standing about and a couple of women. Some of them ignored us and continued eating and drinking, but more and more of them began looking out at us as we passed.

The tavern itself was on the street level of an ordinary daub and wattle building similar to the hovels along the street. Above the low ceiling of the tavern's main drinking area was a floor where the tavern keeper's family probably lived and the tavern girls took their customers. And above that floor there was what appeared to be some kind of storage room. The parish church the protection gang served was several blocks further on down the street.

A log supporting the peaked roof over the tavern's storage room stuck out from the front of the building. There was a rusty pulley attached to it for when bales and barrels of goods and supplies needed to be hauled up to the storage room or lowered from it. The pulley looked like it had not been used for years.

In other words, the tavern was in a building that was quite ordinary for that part of the city, albeit a bit bigger and shabbier. As such, it was quite similar in many ways to the hovels along the sometimes dirt and sometimes stoned street on which we walked. The only differences being that it was larger and had a number of street level window openings whose shutters had been thrown open to let in light. The open shutters let people in the street see into the dimly lit tavern and the people in the tavern see out.

It was, in a word, exactly how Peter Lane and several of the prisoners had described it to me.

"Move further back, lads. We want to form a line with all the windows and the door inside it. ... Go back a little more. ... A little more. ... You too sergeant. We want to give the people in the tavern enough room so they can come out to see what is happening.

"Good. Now remember, lads we are going to let any women and children who come out escape through our ranks unharmed. But not a single one of the men in the tavern is to pass through our line even if you have to kill them to stop them."

There was quite a bit of activity inside the tavern by the time my men were in place. A number of men in the tavern were now clustered around the window openings and door looking out at us. They knew something was up, but they were unsure about what was happening.

A handful of women were in the tavern and looking out as well. Several of them, the women not the men, shouted questions at us and made unfriendly gestures. They shouted at us in Italian so we, of course, could not understand a word they were saying. One man, perhaps the tavern keeper or one of the braver members of the gang, came all the way out of the tavern's door to get a better look at us. *It is strange that it is the women who are so feisty and the men so restrained. I wonder why.*

People in the street outside the tavern saw the grim expressions on our archers' faces, and the way they were holding their swords and longbows, and began backing away. The street was soon empty except for a band of eight or nine ragged and curious young boys. The window openings of the rooms above the street, on the other hand, were full of people.

I looked at the line of archers one last time to make sure the men were in their positions and ready. They were. So I turned and offered a cynical smile to the men inside the tavern, and gave a slight bowing motion with my head and my hand to indicate they were welcome to come out for a look.

By now everyone in the tavern was fully aware of our arrival. The looks on the faces we could see in the dim interior ranged from curious and worried to concerned and downright fearful. Even so, some of them moved nearer to the windows and the door so they could see better, and several of them stepped far enough out of the door to emerge blinking into the bright sunlight.

One thing was clear—most of the people in the tavern still had not a clue as to who we were or what was about to happen. That was no surprise since even my men did not know for sure why we were there. Hopefully some of the tavern goers were innocent local working men who had ended up in the wrong place at the wrong time. They would be amongst those we would try to leave alive if there was fighting. *Which I did not want.*

I did not wait to see how the men in the tavern would respond to my unspoken offer; I nodded my head towards James Howard, and made a motion with my hand, that sent him running to get the wagons. Abraham, Ezra's messenger, remained by my side. So did Peter Lane and the galley's drummer and the horn blower. The archers were in a great semi-circle around the tavern with their bows strung and arrows nocked. The lieutenants had their swords drawn.

The street had become very quiet except for the small band of ragged boys, one of whom was trying to attract attention by strutting up and down and pretending to blow on a horn. No one else on the street was doing anything to draw attention to himself. The only other things moving about were a couple of pigeons pecking at the street stones in front of the tavern and a scrawny cat that had appeared out of nowhere.

Chapter Nine

Vengeance.

The archers watched intently as James led the horse pulling the wagon carrying our sailors to where I was standing in front of the tavern. He kept coming until the horse reached me and I was able to pet the side of the horse's neck. As a result, my hand smelled like the horse and the wagon it was pulling came to a halt directly in front of the tavern's door.

"Use that spar for the ropes, lads."

I gave the order to the three sailors standing in the wagon as I pointed up at the central roof beam that extended out over the tavern's entrance door.

They knew what I wanted and got to work immediately.

Twice a casting stick with a thin line attached to it was underhanded up to the protruding beam. The first cast barely missed, but the second went nicely over it. One of the sailors jumped down from the wagon and grabbed up the stick where it had fallen to the ground. He immediately began hauling on the thin line which, in turn, pulled a heavier rope attached to it up and over the protruding beam and back down.

Three more casting lines followed; two would be used to pull up additional ropes; the third to pull up one of the galley's rope ladders.

What was going to happen next finally began to dawn on the intently watching archers. First one archer, then another, figured it out and began sharing his thoughts with his mates. Soon they were all chattering away to each other with many smiles of agreement and much pointing.

"Silence in the ranks," a lieutenant finally ordered. "Stand firm, damnit."

The response of the people in the tavern when they began to understand was exactly the reverse. They began whispering to each other with looks of disbelief and worry on their faces.

It was a fine spring day. More pigeons had
arrived and were walking about and pecking at the
grass growing between cobblestones and the piles of
horse and human shite which had been deposited on
it by the people of Rome and their visitors.

******

Nothing was said, but everyone knew for sure
what was going to happen when the sailors' wagon
was moved out of the way and the wagon carrying
the prisoners was moved up to take its place.

The wagon full of prisoners, the one with the
Antonio's body and the tightly bound prisoners
stacked on top of one another, came to a halt right
under the overhanging pulley. The prisoners were
quiet except for a few moans and groans.

When the prisoners were first being tied up,
they had cried out most pitiful and made much noise,
especially the wounded ones. Their cries and pleas
had been repeated when they were thrown into the
wagon and stacked up like logs on top of one another.
Now, however, the noise they were making had
quieted down to a few moans that could only be
heard by if someone was standing next to the wagon.

Perhaps it was quieter because those on the bottom of the pile had been unable to breath and were no longer with us. If so, they were probably fortunate. Some of our men had been killed or wounded. The bible and our company's charter required vengeance. It was about to begin.

"Hang the dead one first, Sergeant Atkins. Haul him all the way up to the pulley, and then tie him off well away from the opening so it will be difficult to take him down."

Sailors are inevitably good with ropes and knots. Ours were no exception. They quickly tied a noose at the end of the rope dangling down and got it around Antonio's neck. It was easy for them to do because his body had been deliberately placed on top of the stack of prisoners so they could easily get to it.

Hauling Antonio all the way up, however, turned out not be as easy as it sounded even though the three sailors were highly experienced and had raised many a sail.

The problem was that the rope was laying over the rough piece of protruding wooden roof beam instead of running through the pulley attached to it. The three sailors could not pull hard enough to move the rope over the beam once the full weight of the dead man held the rope against the wood.

Jerking the rope back and forth and adding a file of archers to help the sailors pull solved the problem, and up Antonio went. As soon as he was all the way up to the beam and swinging above them, the sailors pulled a rope ladder up to the beam and one of them scurried up it put another noose around Antonio's neck and tied it directly to the end of the protruding beam.

When that task was finished, the original rope around his neck, the one that had been used to haul him up, was loosened so it could drop to the ground—which left the late and greatly lamented leader of the parish's protection gang tied to the end of the protruding pole and swinging far above the street for all to see. And he was tied at the end of the protruding timber so he could not be cut down by someone reaching out from inside the storage room

"There, by God," I said loudly and with a great deal of satisfaction as the original rope fell to the ground under his swaying body. "They will not get him down easily, will they?"

"Now hang the two live ones from this gang next to him."

******

Everyone in the tavern had recognized Antonio even though his body was quite bedraggled from being wounded and questioned, and then spending a few hours in the river. We could hear a great deal of cursing and muttering as he was hauled up to dangle far above the tavern's entrance.

The distress of the people in the tavern increased even more when they recognized the two live prisoners, and it rose even further when our sailors put nooses around their necks. There were loud screams and shouts from inside the tavern when their begging and pleading suddenly stopped as the sailors and their helpers began hauling them up to dangle next to Antonio.

Once that was done, and the two wounded men had stopped their kicking and pooping, it was time for me to explain the facts of life to the surviving gang members and their neighbours.

I walked towards the tavern entrance with our shipping post's interpreter, and stopped when I thought I was close enough so everyone inside could hear me. Then I loudly began to tell the men inside the tavern how their lives were going to change. My men and Ezra's messenger, Abraham, listened as I did. So did the people in the tavern as the interpreter repeated my words.

"All of you in the tavern listen carefully. Your lives and futures depend on it.

"I am an English archer from the company whose shipping post is just down the street. It was my galley that your parish's protection gang attacked and attempted to rob yesterday. They did so in an effort to get a couple of chests of coins that we were bringing to the Holy Father and the Church.

"My men and I have thrown the bodies of the men we killed into the river and we have just hanged some of the members of your gang we captured. We did so because they attacked the Church and the Holy Father. We also did so because our company's charter, on which every man in the Company of Archers has made his mark, requires great vengeance and serious compensation when one of our men is killed or injured.

"Unfortunately for you who are in the parish's protection gang and still alive, some of our men were killed and wounded in the attack and the Church and Holy Father disrespected. So now you must either pay or every one of you, without exception, will be chopped down or hung.

"But first I am going to tell you why the leaders of your parish's protection gang were stupid even before they ordered you to rob the Pope's coins. Then, I am going to tell you what those of you in the gang who are still alive must do to save yourselves— and what will happen to each and every one of you if you do not do exactly what I say.

"As you know, your gang's captain tried, and failed, to collect a monthly fee from our shipping post which is located nearby. It was foolish of him to even try because our local post captain has no coins of his own to pay, and if he had used the company's coins, even once, he would have been immediately demoted and replaced such that the payments would have stopped. As it is, he is in trouble for not having you all immediately killed." *He was not in trouble, and I will tell him so; but it was a good story.*

"An even better reason for you to never try again to collect a protection fee from the English

Archers' company or rob the Pope, I think you will agree, is this—we know who you are and where to find you. So listen carefully and take heed. Your lives depend on it.

"The next time any one of your gang speaks ill of the Pope, or tries to steal something that belongs to him, or a member of my company or our shipping post is attacked or threatened, we will return and kill every man we find in this tavern. Every man here and in our company is so pledged.

"Finally, your protection gang is to immediately begin paying a gold bezant coin, or its equivalent in silver or copper, to the captain of our shipping post on the first Sunday of each month from now until forever. Failure to do so on or before that day will result in every man in this parish's gang being immediately hunted down and killed most horrible.

"Oh yes, I forgot. There is one more thing. If those coins are ever not paid on time, the captain of the next English galley that calls in at Rome will be under orders to tear this tavern apart, and burn the wood in the street with your bodies on top of the woodpile. The same death and destruction will occur if the bodies hanging over the entrance are cut down before Easter day."

And with that I turned around and we marched off to visit Ezra and more of the gangs which attacked us. My men were very pleased.

Did you notice how I tied what I was doing to defending the Church and the Pope? I thought it a nice touch to keep the Pope sweet as we exacted our revenge. My father and Uncle Thomas would be proud.

******

Abraham guided us to the walled compound where Ezra lived with his family. The compound surprised me in several ways. First, because it was in a very foul and rundown section of the city. Second, because once inside the crumbling wall, I could see that it was actually quite nice with stone floors and wooden shutters on the window openings. And third, because it was full of men from Ezra's company and their families. They were there to help him mourn the death of his son. I could tell they were from his company because they were all wearing their company's little black caps on the back of their heads.

The archers waited outside whilst I went inside with James accompanying me and Abraham leading the way. The place was so packed with mourners from Ezra's company. They were all talking so energetically that it would have been hard to walk about without bumping into someone or being hit with a hand that was waving about to help someone make a point.

One after another everyone went silent and turned to look at us as we entered. Ezra's messenger had hurried on ahead once he had pointed out the entrance the family's compound. As a result, Ezra and the mourners already knew about the fate of the men we had hung less than an hour earlier—and from their smiles and welcoming nods it was clear that they approved of what we had done and appreciated it.

Ezra and two of his sons were waiting at the door to greet me. They were clearly bereaved, but very warm and welcoming as they accepted my heartfelt condolences with handshakes, great manly hugs, and friendship kisses on both sides of our faces.

After I had spent a few minutes being made welcome by various and sundry of the mourners, many of whom were merchants and spoke crusader French, Ezra took my arm and led me down a dimly lit corridor to a small room where we could talk. James Howard and Ezra's two sons came with us.

We got down to business after both of his sons once again reached out to clasp my hand and announced his appreciation and gratitude. They did so in a gobble I could not understand but whose intent was clear and seemed to involve some sort of swearing. One of them was particularly intense to the point of tears. It moved me, and so surprised me that it did, that I had to wait for a moment before I could finally begin.

"There was a leak somewhere, Ezra. Someone let the word out about the coins you and your friends tried to bring to the river yesterday. It could have come from the handful of archers who accompanied me to visit you and overheard us talking, but that is not likely. It is much more likely to have come from someone you know or from the Church." *He looks terrible. Losing his son was a terrible blow.*

"I agree, George. You are right. Your thinking and mine, and the thinking of my friends, are the same. The prisoners we took at the church were too low in rank to know who gave their gang its orders. About the only thing we learnt before we killed them was that they were all members of one of several of the gangs of church toughs that offer "protection" to the merchants and residents in each parish." *Already*

*killed them? Damn. I wanted to talk to them and get
more names for my lists.*

"Well, I brought you some of the prisoners we
took at the river, the ones I have already questioned.
I was going to take them to their parishes and hang
them to encourage the others. But I am running out
of time. So you can have a couple of the live ones if
you want to talk to them. I will keep the rest. I have
plans for them.

"Perhaps you can find out more than I did if you
question them again. In any event, I do not need
them returned since we still have a dozen or so
prisoners left to question back at the river. Hopefully,
we will know even more after I get back to the river
and have a chance to talk to them."

"I am sure you will learn more, George, I am
sure you will. And we will be making serious inquiries
of our own, including from the men you were kind
enough to bring to me. There were too many people
involved for the names of those responsible not to
come out sooner or later. And when they do, my
vengeance will be terrible."

"As will ours, Ezra, as will ours. You can count
on it. We were able to get back to the river in time to

save our coins; has there been any word about who attacked you and got away with most of yours?"

"Not directly, George, not directly. But the attackers I questioned were quite helpful before they died. What they told me ties in nicely with the names of the men on your list and their gang affiliations. There is no doubt in my mind that the raids were carefully coordinated. I think I am beginning to understand who was behind them and why."

At first I was surprised when Ezra told me who he thought was behind the attacks, and even more surprised when he told me why he thought we had been attacked. But the more we talked about what we had heard from our prisoners, and the more I thought about it, the more I agreed with him. We also agreed that we would soon know if our suspicions were true.

But what we did not know is what would happen if we were right. And it was not was not at all what we expected.

Chapter Ten

Visiting a church.

The funerals, our visit to the gang's tavern, and my discussions with Ezra and the transfer of three of the live prisoners had taken much longer than I expected. As a result, it was already well into the afternoon by the time my men and I took our leave of Ezra and headed to our next destination.

The lateness of our leaving was significant. It meant we would not be able to visit the gang hangouts of the prisoners remaining in the wagon until the next day. Accordingly, I got a couple of skins of water off Ezra and told the sailors who were riding in the wagon to periodically give a drink to each of the prisoners in the wagon who was still alive.

I did not order the prisoners to be watered because I was feeling less revengeful or my resolve was weakening. Quite the contrary, I was more furious than ever, particularly after talking to Ezra and seeing his distress at the death of his son. Accordingly, I decided to keep our prisoners alive for a while longer so we could make maximum use of their deaths when we hung them.

Up until today, so far as I was concerned, hanging murderous robbers and pirates up for everyone to see after they were already dead seemed a sufficient warning to everyone to leave us alone. But I had come to realize, as a result of watching the response we had gotten at the tavern a few hours earlier, that it would be better to hang them whilst they were still alive.

It seems that hanging men who are already dead does not impress people as much as hanging them whilst they are pleading for their lives and then kicking and pooping at the end of a rope.

And that is why I ordered our prisoners watered—because I wanted to hang as many of them as possible whilst they were still alive and kicking.

On the other hand, any priests, and particularly any high-ranking priests, who had helped organize the attacks or participated in them, would probably have to have a different fate since I was not sure how the

Church and the Holy Father would react if we hung them publicly. But there was no need to take any chances—we would finish them off privately and make sure that they quietly disappeared.

The importance of hanging robbers and pirates whilst they were still alive had not been taught to me in Uncle Thomas's school. It was a significant deficiency in my formal education, and I put a thought behind my eyes to mention it the next time I scribed a parchment to him.

******

Ezra had confirmed what I now knew to be the case as a result of questioning some of our prisoners—that the priests of each church, and especially its highest-ranking priest, would know if its protection gang was involved in a major raid. They would know because the Church had a rigorous chain of command just as our company did.

Each church's highest ranking priest would know because the leader of his church's protection gang would not dare to participate in a major raid without his approval—and that was particularly significant because each church in Rome was headed by a cardinal who would be close to the Pope as a result of his high rank.

In any event, and perhaps as a result of knowing the importance of the man we were going after, Ezra insisted on sending one of his men, "to help guide you through Rome's streets and translate for you in case you have to speak with the church's servants or any of the local people in its parish."

Ezra made the offer when I told him where we would be going after we left his compound—the Church of Saint Angelo's, the church whose protection gang men we had just hung. The name of the man he proposed to send with us was Pietro. He had eyes that never smiled and was uncommonly tall for an Italian.

I agreed to have Pietro accompany us even though my men and I already knew where the Church of Saint Angelo was located. It was near our shipping post and we had just visited the tavern which was frequented by the men of its protection gang.

What Ezra really wanted, of course, was someone he trusted to report back what happened when we reached Saint Angelo's. I agreed to let his man accompany us because Ezra was a good friend of the company and I wanted to keep him sweet.

According to Ezra, the Church of Saint Angelo was led, as were all the churches in and around Rome, by a cardinal who had been given the parish as his source of coins so the Pope would not have to pay him for his services in helping to run the Church as a whole.

Saint Angelo's, according to Ezra, was the fief of one of the Church's less important cardinals, Jacques Nardin. His palazzo was immediately next to the church.

******

My men and I left Ezra's compound on the north side of the city and, with Pietro, James, and Peter Lane walking with me at the head of column, made our way through the streets of Rome. James carried my longbow and his slung over his back. They were unstrung.

Pietro did not stand out from the rest of us. He wore a tunic similar to ours and carried a sheathed sword and a shield similar to those carried by me and my lieutenants. *I think Ezra deliberately clothed and armed Pietro so he would not stand out amongst my men. He was also not wearing the little black cap on the back of his head that would identify him as part of Ezra's company.*

To avoid doing anything that might alert the priests of Saint Angelo's that we were coming for them, we walked quietly and casually along the route we would take if we were walking straight back to where our galleys were tied up along the river. The wagons, as usual, brought up the rear.

Soon after we left Ezra, I commented to James, loudly enough for the men walking behind us to hear, that it "its time to call it a day and go back to the galleys to get something to eat and give the men a well-earned liberty."

As I knew it would, the news that we were heading back to the river and there would be a liberty spread from man to man down the column faster than a crow could fly. The inevitable result was that the men unstrung their bows and began to relax and began to tell yarns to one another as they walked. I even let them stop to piss against the wall of a wine shop and bought a couple of skins that could be passed from man to man as they walked.

In other words, they stopped looking like a column of armed men who were looking for a fight and began looking like a mob of men walking home after work. It was the best I could think to do.

What I hoped, of course, was that any spies who were watching would think we were merely heading back to our galleys.

******

We stopped pretending that we were merely walking home when we were two blocks away from the church. Peter Lane and Pietro were walking next to me on the street which passed through the gate in the city wall.

They looked at each other when we reached a certain cross street, and then, almost at the same moment, both of them said "there" with great emphasis and pointed in the same direction at the same time—the church was two blocks away on a street that ran parallel to the one we were on.

"Column of files, form on me." … String your bows and prepare to move out for a fight. This is not a drill," I roared as I drew my sword.

As I did, I stepped into the middle of the street and held up both of my hands to show the men where I wanted them to form up in front of me.

There was a silent moment that lasted for about one heartbeat. Then the sergeants began roaring and everyone was running. It did not take long.

"Everyone listen up. There is a church two streets from here with a lord's residence next to it. There is a wall around them both. We are going over the wall and pen them inside. Surround both buildings and fight your way into them if possible. Nobody gets out. Kill any man who tries.

"Now follow me."

And with that I pointed my sword down the side street and set off running. Behind me the horn blower began sounding *Attack* and there was a lot of shouting. Pietro and James Howard were right behind me.

******

I always fancied myself as a swift runner. But some of the lads caught up with me before I was half way there. Perhaps it was the weight of the chain shirt I was wearing and the knives on my wrists that slowed me down, but I doubt it even though they made a fine excuse.

"Keep going," I shouted as the first of the thrusters caught up with me and I made motion with my free hand for them to keep going. "Go around to the rear and close it off."

Getting to Saint Angelo's Church did not take long at all. It came into sight almost immediately, along with the cardinal's residence next to it and the stone wall that surrounded them both. The wall was about five as high as a very short man.

I kept right on running all the way around the wall until I reached a gate. Six or seven speedy runners had beaten me to it—and were waiting for someone to tell them what to do.

"In you go lads. We want to pen them in."

I gave the order just as I reached for the gate and shook it with a push and then a pull. It did not budge.

"Over the wall, lads and open it from the inside." ... "Here, give me a boost." ... "Good man."

One of the men dropped his bow and clasped his hands together as if he was a squire helping me to get aboard a horse. He gave a mighty upward heave a second or so later when I nodded that I was ready. My left hand was both holding my shield and resting on the top of the wall for balance; my right hand, which was holding my short sword, was just starting to touch his shoulder as he took a deep breath and, a moment later, sent me skyward.

I went upward and landed on the top of the wall, more or less rolled over it, and came down in sort of somersault that ended up with me sitting on my arse and damn lucky not to have stabbed or sliced myself with my sword. I was in the church cemetery.

A moment later a two-striper with a great red beard came somewhat similarly over the top of the wall and banged up against me just as I was struggling to regain my feet.

"Get to that church door and hold it."

I gave the order as I staggered to my feet and pointed my sword at a low door into the rear of the church. It was only twenty or thirty paces away.

Alan came over next at the same time as Sergeant Smith, a big man with the muscular arms of someone who had spend a good deal of time in the trade. Pietro and James were right behind them.

"You there, Sergeant Smith," I shouted as I regained my feet and leaned over to pick up my shield. I had somehow dropped it when I threw my hand out in an effort to break my fall.

"Get the gate open and break into the church. I am going for the palace."

******

Peter Lane, Pietro, and James followed close behind me as I ran towards the cardinal's residence. It was just past the church on the other side of the cemetery. The main entrance and the residence's cook house were obviously on the other side of the building.

We headed at a run for a small door in the side of the stone building. It opened on to dirt path through the cemetery that led to the church. Several archers were running right behind us. It was not certain how the archers had gotten inside the wall, and it did not matter; I was pleased to see them. As a general rule, there is safety in numbers.

The building we were running towards had stone walls and was quite large with at least one additional floor above the ground floor and probably two or even three. It had to be large if the cardinal was to enjoy his comforts in addition to providing housing for his priests, seminarians, and servants.

We were in the rear of the house and could see a door from the cardinal's residence that opened onto a path to the church. If the door was not barred, it would either mean that the cardinal and his guards were not expecting our arrival or that they knew we were coming and were dumber than stones for not barring it.

I tried the door, and it moved when I gave it a little push. So I pushed the door hard and quickly stepped back as it opened into the building. No one was there, but I could hear the faint sound of men shouting from somewhere inside. Our men were probably either in already, or trying to get in, at the main door which opened out towards the street on the other side of the building.

The empty hallway I stepped into had shuttered windows all along one side of its stone wall. I moved cautiously down the narrow corridor with my sword at the ready and my shield up.

James was next to me and Pietro and Peter Lane were right behind us with their weapons similarly prepared. Several archers were behind the four of us along with a lieutenant carrying a sword and shield. The distant shouting continued, but there was no sound of fighting.

All the noise was on the other side of the house. We were instinctively quiet and on high alert as we slowly moved as silently as possible down the narrow corridor in a tight little group.

What we cautiously entered as we crept out of the walkway was an eating hall with wooden tables and benches. It was not a great hall such as one would find in a rich palace like that of the Holy Father's or the Empress's; it was more like the plain hall of a country nobleman with ceilings high enough for a man to stand upright.

There was a fireplace at one end of the hall, the end where we had entered. As might be expected, it had a chimney as befitted the home of a great lord or prince who was dainty enough not to want to eat or receive his guests in a cloud of smoke.

A stone staircase at the other end of the eating hall ran up to whatever rooms were above the ground floor. What made this hall different from the hall of a country lord were the pieces of linen with pictures of Jesus and extremely fat little babies with wings painted on them. They were hanging on the stone walls of the hall to keep out the dangerous night air when the wind was blowing.

My God, do the Italians fatten up their children and eat them? The Rus and Vikings who are still barbarians do, of course, but I would never have believed it of the Italians now that most of them are Christians. It certainly explains why the Church encourages its priests to spend their free time with boys and men instead of marrying and having children.

Chapter Eleven

Priestly Confessions.

James and I barely had time to step into the hall when all hell broke loose. There was a sudden great surge of shouting and the unmistakable sound of many running feet. They were somewhere above us and coming fast.

I took a step backwards and those of us with swords instinctively formed a shield wall in front of the narrow corridor from which we had just emerged. James and the two archers were immediately behind us with the points of their nocked arrows just above our shields and ready to be pushed.

A few seconds later a great gaggle of black-robed young boys began pouring down the stairs at the other end of the hall. They were wild-eyed and running desperately. Many of them were looking back over their shoulders as they ran.

The boys who saw us first were those who were leading the way. Several of them screamed and tried to turn around to go back up the stairs. Unfortunately, the boys behind them kept coming. The result was chaos on the stairs as hysterical and crying boys tripped over each other and fell down.

"Prohibere. Sede. Est Licuit. Nemo vobis nocebit"

Somehow the Latin words out for "Stop. Sit down. No one will hurt you." jumped into my mind as I put down my sword down and stepped forward towards the stairs. I repeated them several times as my hands went up with my palms opened towards them, both to signal the boys to halt and to show them we meant them no harm. They looked to be of varying ages from six or seven years old to fourteen or fifteen. We knew they were young because none of them had beards.

At first the boys just stared at me and the men grouped behind me with wide-eyed and uncertain eyes, probably because of my English accent and our sudden appearance carrying weapons. I had to repeat my order several times whilst making downward motions with my hands. Finally, one after another, they began to sit down on the stairs and along the wall.

Several of the boys were terrified and sobbing, but others were mostly wide-eyed and curious as they began sitting down. Two bearded priests had been bringing up the rear, but they had successfully turned around and run back the way they came. Several of the rear-most boys followed them.

******

We ended up capturing everyone in the building. They ranged from altar boys and young seminarians to priests and a very irate and prissy little cardinal by the name of Jacques Nardin. There was not a woman or girl among them.

I found a room near from main entrance and conducted my questioning there. The men began bringing the priests and the boys to me one at a time. The boys came first. As you might imagine, I questioned them in private in case they revealed something that it was best for the men of the company or the money lenders not to know.

Lieutenant Anderson brought the cardinal to me just as I was finishing an interesting talk with one of the younger lads. I knew instantly that he was the cardinal from the arrogant expression on his face the fur and fine embroidery on the robe he was wearing despite the warmth of the day.

"We found this one hiding in one of those upstanding wooden boxes where the gentry hang their tunics and such, Commander. Behind some priests' robes he was. I shut the door and almost missed him. But then Tommy and I heard him moving about and opened it again."

"Cardinal Jacques Nardin I presume?" I said it in Latin with a smile on my face and a touch of sarcasm and pleasure in my voice. *And rightly so; I was more than a little pleased to have an opportunity to talk with him. Here, so to speak, was an opportunity to get the information we needed directly from the horse's mouth.*

Asking my question to confirm his identity was the first thing I did when the lieutenant brought the cardinal to me. We met in the little room in the front of the building, the room where I had been talking to the boys.

I was ready for him because the boys I had already spoken with were bright lads for the most part and, importantly, several of them had been like flies on the wall when their betters had been talking about attacking us. I had already learnt quite a bit about the cardinal and his friends from the boys and from Ezra, but I had decisions to make and I wanted to know much more before I made them.

"I am *Cardinal* Nardin."

He said it rather imperiously as he emphasized his title and held out his ring to be kissed. I ignored it. But then he cocked his head in a delayed surprise at my question and asked one of his own,

"How is it that you can gobble Latin and know my name, were you once a priest?"

"I still am a priest, Your Eminence—a priest with dispensations so he can lead a normal life, of all things, and one who is loyal to the Pope and the Church." *Well, not in all ways, of course; but certainly whenever it does not conflict with whatever else I am doing.*

"And you, Cardinal Nardin. Are you loyal to the Church and the Holy Father?"

I was fairly sure Cardinal Nardin was *not* loyal to the Pope, both because of his gang's participation in the attack and what I heard from the boys. But I did not want to take a chance by immediately scoffing at him so in the off-chance that he turned out to be an innocent friend, relative, or lover of the Holy Father.

Not that I thought the latter was likely, mind you. It was well known, even beyond Rome, that the Holy Father had gotten several children out of his lady friends and was working on getting more.

"Of course I am loyal to the Church and the Pope," the cardinal replied rather indignantly. "How dare you ask?"

I had already decided not to mention Ezra's name to anyone or that it was two of the boys who told me what they had heard him say to several of his fellow cardinals whilst they were in their wine bowls and discussing the raids.

As a result, I acted as a priest was expected to act when it was necessary to protect the Church or a fellow priest—I lied about what I knew. I did so in case the cardinal lived through the ordeal that was coming and somehow returned to the bosom of the Church.

"Ah, well that is the problem you see. It seems that some of your priests and the men in your parish's protection gang think that you, and others amongst the cardinals and bishops who are your friends and fellow Frenchmen, organized the recent attacks on the English galleys in the river and on the moneylenders. Is that not so?"

"It certainly is not. I have never attacked anyone."

I started to say something sarcastic about the man who orders an attack being worse than the poor sods who were in it because they had no choice. But I did not. Instead, I stifled the urge to challenge him and changed the subject in an effort to get him a bit off balance.

"By the way, Cardinal, and just between us before I start asking the rest of my questions, does the Holy Father know you have been diddling the boys in your seminary and telling them it is part of their duties to serve you because you are a priest? Or would you prefer I not mention it in my report?"

"Report whatever you will. The Holy Father understands such things even though his own personal interests are elsewhere."

"That may be so, but would he understand the efforts of you and your friends to steal his coins?"

Mentioning the coins hit home. The cardinal's eyes narrowed and he looked at me carefully.

"What is it that you want, Father? To be a bishop? Money? Talking to you is wasting my time and I have much to do for the Church. I would rather give you whatever it is that you want so you will take your men and go away."

"Being a bishop would be nice if the diocese was someplace warm such as France," I suggested. "But is it possible?"

"Anything is possible, particularly in France. I am originally from France and have many friends there who are high in the French Church."

"But would that not require the approval of a French archbishop and, quite possibly, the French king himself?"

"Of course it would, but my friends and I have good relations with Louis and the French archbishops. They are very good actually. The Diocese of Arles is available as a matter of fact." *Ezra was right; they are all connected to France.*

"A bishopric in France is available? Well now, that is certainly worth considering. But first there are some questions that need to be answered. And I am afraid I will have to require you to answer them. Now then, I have a list of the cardinals and bishops here in Rome, what I need you to tell...”

The poor fellow got red in the face and became absolutely apoplectic with rage.

“This is absurd. How dare you talk to me like that? I am not going to answer your questions. You are to leave immediately and take your men with you.”

“You know, I thought you might say something like that. And I certainly do wish I could leave. But I cannot go until you answer my questions, which you will now do because of what will happen if you do not.

I leaned forward and asked the first of my many questions with a great deal of threat and intensity in my voice.

“Do you want to know what will happen until you do answer them, or if you lie to me?”

“No, I do know and I do not want to know. What I want is for you to leave.”

I ignored his lack of interest and proceeded to answer the question for him.

"What will happen is that each time you do not answer one of my questions truthfully I will cut off one of your fingers or one of your ballocks. And when I question the rest of your priests and fellow cardinals and bishops, which I will, and find out that you have told me even one lie, I will cut off your dingle and slice your lips so your mouth opens twice as wide."

Cardinal Nardin was clearly taken aback and stunned. It was likely no one had spoken to him like that for years.

"Ha," he said after he thought about what I had said for awhile. And then a look triumph and realization filled his face.

"You cannot touch me. I am a priest and a cardinal. Harming a priest is forbidden by both God and the Church. I can do anything I want. And right now what I want is for you to leave."

The cardinal still had a triumphant look on his face when I suddenly reached out and firmly grabbed a finger on his right hand with my left hand. The wrist knife on my right hand came out in the blink of an eye with the speed one might expect from someone who had practiced bringing it out every day for a good many years. And, without even pausing, I promptly sliced off his pointing finger at the second joint.

Cardinal Nardin pulled back what was left of his hand and looked at it in amazement and disbelief, and then he looked at me and watched as I casually tossed his missing finger on the floor, and then he began screaming. He also began bleeding quite profusely as is always the case in such matters.

"It would appear that God and the Church have withdrawn their protections from you, and rightly so. Robbing and killing innocent people will do that for a man almost every time. Now you will tell me everything, yes?"

Chapter Twelve
Time to set our sails.

What I learned from Cardinal Nardin was that it was the Church's French bishops and cardinals who had ordered the attacks, and that a certain Cardinal Bouvier was their leader and had organized them.

I also learned that the French cardinals and bishops were stronger and more dedicated than anyone would have expected. Not dedicated to God and the Church, of course, but dedicated to moving the papacy to France so that God would speak to the faithful through a Pope with a French accent when he told them what they must do.

According to Cardinal Nardin, he and his fellow French cardinals and bishops were displeased because Italian priests got most of the Church's plum appointments and riches. And since they were never given the riches and recognition they believed they deserved, they had decided to change the Church and take them.

In essence, according to the now-babbling cardinal, the raids were intended to weaken the Holy Father's finances, and provide the coins the French clerics would need to buy enough votes from the Italian cardinals to move the papacy to France.

And, in the event such a move proved temporarily impossible, the Empress's coins would be used so they would not have to wait to live in the style to which they intended to become accustomed when the papacy did move to France.

It was a great folly, of course, because the Italian cardinals would never elect a non-Italian Pope, and an Italian Pope would never agree to move to France. On the other hand, the efforts of the French cardinals and bishops to buy the papacy would keep them busy in the years ahead—and so would we; they and their Venetian allies had become the mortal enemies of my company by killing some of our men.

******

Questioning Cardinal Nardin and his priests, and also their boys and servants, took up all the rest of the day and continued by candlelight until well after dark. Then we tied the arms and legs of the pain-wracked cardinal and several of his priests together, stacked them in the wagon with the rest of our prisoners, and took them with us to our galleys. They did not know it yet, but they had attacked their last Englishman.

I made number of decisions as we made our way back to the river in the darkness. For one, I decided to leave the fate of the rest of the French gangs and priests to Ezra. Summer was coming and I had found myself thinking of my women and our children more and more. It was time to carry the Pope's decree to Constantinople, and then set our sails for England with the Empress's coins that remained after those required by the Holy Father had been collected.

Accordingly, I scribed a somewhat misleading parchment for Ezra suggesting that the attacks had been ordered by Cardinal Nardin and organized by some his priests and the leader of his protection gang. I also informed him that to atone for their sins against the Holy Father and the Church they had agreed to accompany me on a pilgrimage to pray in the Holy Land despite the many great dangers inherent in such a voyage.

As you might imagine, I said no more. If I had told Ezra about the involvement of the other French cardinals and bishops, he would have felt obliged to revenge his son and his lost coins by killing them; if I had warned the Pope about the evil intentions of his French cardinals, he would have gotten irate and cast them out of the Church.

And if either of those things happened there would have been no French churchmen left to encourage the Venetians, the Latin nobles, and the Orthodox lords to move against Constantinople—and then the Empress would no longer need us and there would be fewer refugees.

Earning coins is too important to let one's emotions get in the way of earning them. At least, that is what my father always said. Besides, now that I know who wronged us, we can pick them off one at a time.

End of the Book

There are more books in the *Company of Archers* saga.

All of the other books in this great saga of medieval England are available as eBooks, and most of them are available in print. Some are also available as audio books. You can find them by going to Amazon or Google and searching for *Martin Archer fiction*.

Additional eBook collections of the novels in the saga are available on Kindle as *The Archers' Story: Part I, Part II, Part III, Part VI, and Part V.* And there are more stories after those. A chronological list can be found below.

And a word from Martin:

"Thank you for reading my stories. I sincerely hope you enjoy reading about Cornwall's *Company of Archers* as much as I enjoy writing about them. If so, would you please consider writing a very brief review on Amazon or Google or Goodreads with as many stars as possible in order to encourage other readers.

"And, if you could please spare a moment, I would also very much appreciate your thoughts about this saga of medieval England and whether you would like it to continue. I can be reached at martinarcherV@gmail.com."

Cheers and thank you once again. /S/ Martin Archer

Amazon eBooks in Martin Archer's exciting and action-packed *The Company of Archers* saga:

The Archer

The Archers' Castle

The Archers' Return

The Archers' War

Rescuing the Hostages

Kings and Crusaders

The Archers' Gold

The Missing Treasure

Castling the King

The Sea Warriors

The Captain's Men

Gulling the Kings

The Magna Carta Decision

The War of the Kings

The Company's Revenge

The Ransom

The New Commander

The Gold Coins

The Empires Gold

Fatal Mistakes

The Alchemist's Revenge

The Venetian Gambit

Today's Friends

The English Gambit

Amazon eBooks in Martin Archer's exciting and action-packed *Soldier and Marines* saga:

Soldier and Marines

Peace and Conflict

War Breaks Out

Our Next War

Our inspection of the city's outer defensive wall took us in a big circle. First, we rode easterly through temporary gaps in the enclosures *inside* the city's moat-fronted outer defensive wall all the way to where the end of the wall met the water of the estuary called, for some reason I never understood, "The Golden Horn." Whatever its strange name, it was important because much of the city's food came down the two big rivers that came out of the Empire's lands and emptied into it.

When we reached the waters of the estuary at the eastern end of the outer wall, we turned around and rode back westerly all the along the *outside* of the outer wall's moat until we reached the waters of the Marmara Sea on the western side of the peninsula. From the western end of the wall we rode back easterly through the enclosures until we got back to where we began.

The entire ride took about three hours because the total outer defensive wall looked to be about ten thousand paces long and we stopped periodically along the way to talk about possible weak points where more work was needed. I particularly pointed out where the slivers of land between the moat and the outer wall needed to blocked so the attackers could not get across the moat and then run down along the outside of the wall with ladders and climb over it in numerous places.

If the attackers could do that, they would be in a number of enclosures and could begin attacking the city's inner defensive wall from multiple points at the same time. Our goal, I said, was to keep any attackers who got over or through the city's outer wall jammed together in one or two enclosures so our archers could stand on the walls around them and shoot them down.

I also explained that holding the inner and outward walls where the archers would be concentrated was the key to winning the war because the city was at the very end of a long and narrow peninsula which stuck out into the Marmara Sea. The other three sides of the city, I told them, were only protected by a single wall around them. But it was mostly built so close to the sea that it would be much more difficult for an invader to successfully attack.

Read more of *Fatal Mistakes*. It is available exclusively on Amazon in print, as an e-book, and can be read for free in the Kindle lending library. The *Alchemist's Revenge* is the book that follows *Fatal Mistakes*.

9 798684 208508